FOLLOW THE SUN

Sapphire Cay, book 1

RJ SCOTT

MEREDITH RUSSELL

Love Lane Books

Copyright

Dedication

For our family and friends

SAPPHIRE CAY 1

FOLLOW THE *Sun*

RJ SCOTT &
MEREDITH RUSSELL

Chapter One

"WE WANT YOU IN PLACE BY THE FOURTH OF NEXT MONTH and no later." Oscar Morgan was not beating around the bush. His words were brusque, final, and brooked no argument.

Lucas Madison swallowed the sudden feelings of claustrophobia and panic—quickly calculating how much time that gave him. Two weeks on the island, and then he would need to return straight to the office. He closed his eyes against the bright sun and shifted in the waiting room seat until his five-ten frame was finally in a comfortable position. That wasn't enough time to get his head straight.

"That's a bit tight," he said. Choosing his words carefully was his stock in trade these days. React too aggressively and Oscar would see he wasn't as committed as he used to be. Lucas had to toe the company line and stay focused despite the fact his head was at direct odds with his heart, which was telling him to just walk away.

Oscar tutted. *What?* Why the tutting? Did he think there was any other response Lucas could give? The deadline *was* tight—what did Oscar want him to do? Magically prepare contracts and negotiate terms? Lucas bit his tongue and began to count back from ten.

"Johnson not being here to cover you is hard enough," Oscar began. Lucas closed his eyes. The grief over losing his friend was still fresh. Oscar mentioning Alan's name as if dying at fifty-three was an inconvenience served to do nothing except cut the wound open again. His boss was still talking and Lucas forced himself to listen. "I'm not entirely convinced the new rep, Patterson, can handle the west coast as much as we had hoped. You need to get in there before he does more damage than you can fix."

A mix of emotions washed over him at the words 'West Coast'. Ever since Alan Johnson, Lucas's friend and mentor and the existing West Coast manager, had keeled over in the parking lot after his youngest boy's ball game, the general consensus was that Lucas would be the new manager on that side of the US. Alan had two kids in college, so much to look forward to, and at fifty-three, he was too young to have died. They said he had a stroke and that his body just gave up but Lucas knew better; Morgan Municipal had killed his friend.

Lucas hadn't known where to turn since Alan was gone. The company had insisted, in some kind of corporate panic following Alan's death, that all employees get physicals at their own expense—just to make sure no one else died on their books. Lucas hadn't been worried about his physical. He'd passed his first one for the company at twenty-two with flying colors and this time would surely be no different. He was thirty-two, not sixty-two, and he was fit. Not a gym rat by any stretch of the imagination, but he was healthy.

The news he had been given had been enough to knock everything into perspective. He may well have investments, a nearly mortgage-free house, and a growing pension, but he also had eighteen-hour work days. All the plans for the future paled next to what he had been told. If he didn't stop, he was dead. Simple. Ulcers and high blood pressure were slowly killing him.

"I'll be there on the fourth," Lucas said carefully. He'd be there to negotiate fewer hours and more support. The constant nagging tension in his chest spiked in a sharp pain. Friends warned him that working eighteen-hour days six, sometimes seven days a week was going to end up killing him. They didn't need to warn him anymore; doctors had done a very good job of cutting short the future laid before him.

Glancing over at his sister, he caught her glaring back at him. He didn't blame her for her reaction. After all, she didn't know what was wrong, and why would he tell her? This was her wedding and he had spent ten years caring for his sister and shielding her from the bad things in life. He wasn't about to stop now. He had promised her he wouldn't be on his phone every hour God sent, but receiving this call from Morgan himself wasn't something he could ignore. This last job would bring in enough money to tide him over for a year. He wouldn't need to touch his extensive savings and investments. Just one more job and then he'd take some time off.

Tasha was still staring, but there was a new expression

on her face. A thoughtful, lost look of sadness that he had put there.

Oscar's voice was still in his ear. "This contract needs negotiations; Patterson has already messed up on most of it. You need to go in there, negotiate with the partners, make them an offer, and stick by it."

"Is he getting any backup?" Patterson had been headhunted into Morgan Municipal as a bright young thing. A small sense of satisfaction washed over Lucas when he heard Patterson was fucking things up, but then he felt immediately guilty. Patterson was a nice man and reminded Lucas of what he had been like ten years ago: full of enthusiasm for his career and aiming for a bright future.

"He's a liability," Morgan said. "Can't even negotiate a decent contract in our favor. He's too damn nice for his own good. Between you and me, I'm considering having his papers drawn up this morning to let him go as soon as you're back on US soil. You'll be flying straight from Miami to Sea-Tac. I'll have Anna arrange the flights. I'm emailing you the files for the negotiation that Patterson fucked up; I'll need them back in ten days to pass through the steering group." So casually, the boss decided that Patterson was a liability. Patterson had been good for Lucas, lessening the time he was needed in the office. Yes, he was new and somewhat inexperienced, but his input had made a work-life balance possible for Lucas. And now his boss was removing that crutch entirely? One more thing to tip the balance for Lucas to just up and leave.

Ten days. Lucas thought about what the next week and a half held for him. A wedding rehearsal and meal, the wedding itself. That left the rest of what he was supposed to be calling a vacation. He could clear the contract files left for him if he could just get a solid ten-hour day in somewhere. One more contract finished and he could ride the bonus on it for a year. Get some rest. Get well.

Tasha would have to understand without him explaining fully what he was doing. As long as he was there next to her when she walked down the aisle, or whatever people did on beach weddings, then he was sure she would be fine. He would have done his brotherly duties and seen Tasha marry. Maybe then he could slip in a bit of work. She'd be preoccupied with Liam and being all loved up.

"Send it over," Lucas agreed softly. Casually, he glanced up and over at his sister. She wasn't watching him but he could tell she was listening. He knew her too well and braced himself for the tongue lashing that accompanied him disappointing her. She simply looked his way briefly. There was no censure on her expression; instead her eyes held that same incredible sadness.

Lucas bristled but then just as quickly deflated. *Great.* He was in for one of his sister's pity talks. She had to see that not everyone was going to be lucky enough to be part of a 'married with kids, settled for life' scenario; hell, he was gay, as he liked to remind her. It wasn't part of the hand he'd been dealt. The whole family thing certainly hadn't worked out for Alan, nor was it looking so hot for Patterson.

"Lucas? You still there?"

Lucas snapped back to concentrating on the person at the other end of the phone. "Sorry. Bad line."

His boss tutted his disapproval again. "Damned inconvenient, you leaving on a vacation at this point."

His sister's wedding wasn't really a vacation and he couldn't and *wouldn't* let Tasha down. His sister was the only family he had since he became her guardian at twenty-two when she had just turned seventeen. She wanted two full weeks on an island retreat to get married, and she wanted her brother to stop his life just for those two weeks. He would do anything for her. She'd always wanted a big wedding, but Lucas had always imagined a white dress and a church somewhere in their home city of Seattle. Setting the wedding on Sapphire Cay in the Bahamas, only accessible by boat and as far away from civilization as it was possible to get, was a shock. As far as he remembered, she was always dressing her Barbies in white and making churches out of cardboard boxes.

He even recalled the day he announced Ken was actually gay, which had sent Tasha into a tailspin of temper. His mom had calmed them down, but when he was fourteen and Tasha was nine, he already knew devious ways of bypassing his mom's talks. He wasn't even entirely sure at that point that he had known what gay was. Nope, that revelation hit him in the face with enough force to send him to his knees when he turned fifteen. Being appreciative on gym days of his friends' bodies and being entirely not interested in the blooming of boobs had kind of been the nail in the proverbial coffin. He was gay. He wasn't going to get married and have two kids and a dog and a freaking minivan. He was going to find his success and fulfillment in a different way.

"My sister is getting married," Lucas explained.

There was another huff and then his boss simply confirmed the files had been mailed and ended the call.

Lucas pocketed his phone and casually looked around for some kind of sign that proclaimed internet access. He couldn't see anything in the immediate area and he stood and stretched tall.

"What are you doing?" Tasha asked suspiciously. He had been sure she was looking the other way; she had eyes in the back of her head that one.

"Going to look for the bathroom," Lucas said evenly. With a smile, he sauntered away from her and her fiancé and the rest of his sister's friends. He didn't really know any of them but guessed they were here as support. That and a vacation.

He passed the welcome desk and checked the arrival time for their water taxi from Marsh Harbor to Sapphire Cay. According to the schedule, he had another forty minutes. Plenty of time to find a computer, locate the email, and print off the supposed clusterfuck that Patterson had created. Then he could maybe look at it on the boat and slip it out as and when he had time.

Paperwork downloaded and printed—all forty-seven pages—and with a smile of thanks from the administrator who was now holding eighty dollars in his hands, Lucas pushed the papers into his flight bag and made his way back to his sister.

"You've been gone half an hour," she said with a sigh.

"Was exploring. Killing time," he lied again. He was getting good at this lying thing.

"Why did you take your bag?"

"I didn't want you to worry about it."

"You're working aren't you?" She stood up with frustration in her eyes.

"I'm not."

"Lucas, I can see right through you." This time the frustration was tinged with sadness and resignation.

"Leave it, Tasha. Okay?" Stress built inside him. It was *his* hard work that had put her through college so she could get a decent job, and it was *his* money helping her to hire a freaking island to get married on, so she should hold off on commenting on his life. Or lack of it.

Jeez. Where had that thought come from? She was his sister and just worried about him. He was the one fucking everything up. She'd been the first person to be there when Alan died, the only one outside of Alan's family who knew just how much the man meant to him. Alan's kids called him Uncle, and Rosemary, Alan's wife of over thirty years, knew all his favorite dinners.

"We need to move to the quayside. The boat will be ready to go in ten," Liam interrupted the brother-sister face-off diplomatically. His sister's fiancé was good at that. Lucas could feel Tasha's guests staring at them, and embarrassment crawled inside him. Carefully, he turned away and grabbed the handle of his rolling suitcase. With that and his flight bag, he was ready to go and the discussion was diverted. Tasha was distracted by getting her bags and the argument was shelved. Lucas doubted it would be forgotten. Finally, they were all standing at the quayside after locating the mooring for the Sapphire Cay boat, curiously called *Lady Liberty*.

"Come aboard." A man was waiting for them and holding out his hand to help each person onto the wide-open and frankly flimsy-looking boat. When it was Lucas's turn, he first passed on his luggage and the captain placed it with the other bags. Concentrating on seeing his bag was placed in the right area, he stumbled as he climbed in, and the guy had to use some of the muscles he was showing in a cutoff tee and board shorts to steady Lucas. Irritated that he needed help at all, he turned his back to the slightly taller man and focused on finding a seat to the side of the small boat. Finally, he was seated just in front of a redhead, who kept talking about the kids she had left with her mom, and her partner, who nodded at everything she said.

He was sitting at an angle to his sister, who grasped Liam's hand like she was never letting go. He liked Liam. Liked him a lot. That was the protective big brother inside him who wanted his sister happy and settled with a good man. Liam was a good man with a solid career in marketing and his own agency.

"Okay. Y'all ready to go?" Tall-guy's voice was melodious, and if Lucas wasn't mistaken there was a hint of the south in the drawled vowels. As everyone else said their yeses, Lucas took the time to appreciate the view. And he didn't mean the crystal blue sea or the vastness of the azure sky. He was focusing on every little detail of their captain, or whatever he called himself.

"Welcome aboard. My name is Dylan." *Well that answers that question.* "I'll be taking you over to the Cay. Just a few things. The trip to Sapphire Cay should take us about fifty minutes. Please no leaning over the side and no jumping off the boat until we're in deeper waters. Just to warn you, we often have heavy rain that lasts for a few minutes and then clears just as quickly, but there are umbrellas in the storage bin at the back." Dylan moved past the guests to the back of the boat and started the small outboard motor. He slipped the rope and soon they were heading away from Marsh Harbor and out into the expanse of ocean.

From his seat, Lucas had a good look at the man who was competently guiding them to the island for the wedding. He was probably an inch or so above his own five ten, and he had the fit, lean body of a swimmer. Lean and muscled and with skin burnished gold by the Bahamian sun, he was a sight for sore eyes. Lucas couldn't remember the last time he had the space to stare at a good-looking guy just for the sake of it. Dylan's hair was a fascinating shade of dark brown shot through with sun-bleached blond strands that hung in soft, shaggy waves around his face. With brightly colored board shorts and a faded pink tee, he was the epitome of beach bum. Lucas spent a good amount of time imagining the color of Dylan's eyes since dark shades hid them. He pictured them the same cornflower blue as the sky or maybe an emerald green like the shallow sea. He was just relieved he could stare from behind his own shades. Dylan wouldn't know. The fifty minutes passed against the background of chattering and lots of oohing and aahing from various passengers. Dylan pointed out schools of blue and green parrot fish. Even Lucas admitted they were stunning as they darted this way and that around the boat, and the shimmer of color was fascinating to see.

They caught their first glimpse of Sapphire Cay as little more than a smudge on the horizon. The smile on

Tasha's face as they drew nearer was one of wonder, and a small part of Lucas melted as he watched her expression. Whatever he had to do while he was here, none of it was as important as seeing his sister happy. He picked at his shirt, pulling it away from his skin and moving it so air hit him. Sweat was pooling at the back of his neck and the base of his spine. Maybe slacks and a shirt were not the most practical of clothing for a boat trip in the Bahamas.

"So, you didn't bring anyone with you?" the redhead with the kids asked him. Clearly, she had run out of stories about toddling and talking and diapers and had turned her attention to her next victim.

"Huh?"

"You're here alone? Is your boyfriend coming over later?"

"I am currently boyfriendless," Lucas responded. Like it was actually possible to have any kind of relationship right now. There was just so much else going on. It wouldn't be fair to him or anyone. Although, why it was any of her business he didn't know. Clearly though, she knew enough about him to feel comfortable with her questions.

"You never know, there may be some cute young thing on the island for you."

Lucas doubted it. Sapphire Cay had about twenty staff, including the owners, and the rest of the population was made up of the guests sitting in the boat and the few others that arrived tomorrow. It didn't make the pool of prospective gay suitors all that big.

"I have too much work to do to look for men," he said.

He regretted the statement when his sister piped up with her usual anti-work refrain.

"Luc is happier taking his work to bed," she said cheekily. Lucas buried his head to stop anyone from seeing the blush of temper at his sister bandying around his personal life. He was a private person and he didn't know these people from Adam. He mumbled something appropriate.

"If you look to your left, you'll see the dock and the hotel now," Dylan interrupted. Lucas was never happier to hear the captain's voice and he looked up to see Dylan looking back at him. There was a curious expression on his face. Puzzlement? Inquiry? A frown? Lucas looked away quickly. He wasn't dealing with what a stranger thought about what he had heard any more than he could be bothered to deal with the rest of the people on the boat.

The hotel was wide, low, and painted white. The building was nestled in amongst greenery, and wide steps led up from the beach. A welcoming party waited on the beach, and with bags off of the boat and his five-hundred dollar shoes sinking in the sand, Lucas followed the rest of the party up the stairs and to the hotel foyer. Crisp and clean and cool, it was a welcome change after having the sun on his back for so long. He just wanted a shower and a drink, most definitely in that order. The captain didn't follow them up into the hotel and Lucas was left to wonder how the man filled his time. Did he stay here on the island between trips or return to the mainland? Probably the latter. Shame. Lucas would have liked to have stared some more.

Chapter Two

CHRIST, HE NEEDED A DRINK. HE HADN'T OFFICIALLY started on any medication yet, happy to put it off until after the weekend. With that in mind, he planned to make the most of it. This could possibly be the last occasion that he and alcohol were joined at the hip. Lucas held the empty champagne flute in his hand and gently tapped his fingers against its rim. The redhead, now formally introduced as Kate, chief and only bridesmaid for his sister, had made it her duty to get to know every detail of his life. He was, after all, father, mother, and brother of the bride all rolled into one. He smiled politely as Kate reeled off another fun fact about his sister. Apparently, she and Tasha went to Vegas last year.

"And there was this man in drag and he was…" She grinned and leaned in close. "Well, I don't need to tell you. I bet you see all kinds of crazy things."

"Crazy things?" He probably shouldn't have asked.

"Well," she said and then lowered her voice as if to tell a secret, "you're gay."

Lucas raised an eyebrow and nodded. "Yes, I am," he said slowly, not entirely sure how that had anything to do with seeing so-called 'crazy things'.

Kate winked and, seemingly content with Lucas's answer, turned back to talk to her husband. This was going to be a long night.

Clearing his throat, Lucas waved a hand in the air. He really needed that drink. He smiled as he met the eyes of the pretty blonde who had been serving the table all night, and she was quickly at his side, filling his glass with champagne. He eyed the back of Kate's head. He'd never met the woman in his life and tried to recall what her connection was to his sister. He remembered there had been a Kate at university—Tasha's second-year roommate. That must be it. To be honest, he knew very few of Tasha's friends. He had always been working, and then a couple of years ago she had moved in with Liam.

"Are you okay?" Tasha asked as she rested her hand over Lucas's. He smiled as her warm fingers circled around his. "I'm so sorry if she's bothering you." She smirked as she leaned forward and looked at Kate.

"It's fine," Lucas lied. The woman was annoying but she had a big heart. She loved her husband, her children, and from the sound of it, she loved Tasha like a sister. "And no, you're not sorry." She'd have done it on purpose. It was her way of making him suffer for even daring to think about working while he was out here. It was a vacation, she had told him several times. A well-deserved one.

Tasha grinned. "She's an acquired taste," she said with a laugh and tucked a strand of her dark blonde hair behind her ear. She seemed to have relaxed since that morning. Stress and nerves had been creeping in over the last few days, but now that she, her husband-to-be, their closest family and friends, and, most importantly, her dress had all arrived safely on the island, she was finally looking forward to her big day. Christ, how was it his baby sister was getting married tomorrow? He had been responsible for her for almost ten years and had proudly watched as she had grown from an annoying seventeen-year-old brat into a fine, dedicated young woman.

Lucas smiled and met his sister's eyes. "So long as she's *your* taste, I really don't mind." He pressed his lips to her temple in a warm kiss. All he wanted was for this weekend to go off without a hitch. Tasha deserved to be happy. He chewed thoughtfully on his lip, and his smile grew wider. It was time to play his part. Getting to his feet, Lucas picked up his glass and fork, chiming them together as he called for attention.

"What are you doing?" Tasha asked in a hushed voice. This was something she hadn't planned on.

"My duty," he said. Taking a deep breath, he looked around the large, circular table and at the eight expectant faces staring back up at him. If this was a meeting for Municipal, he'd have his tablet, projector, PowerPoint presentations filled with charts and data, and his performance would be spot on. Every single thing would be perfect. Pushing his hand into his pants pocket, he did his best to relax.

"Hi," he started, kind of wishing his opening had had a little more impact. "As most of you know, my baby sister is getting married tomorrow." Kate whooped and everyone laughed. "First, I want to thank the staff for a beautiful evening." He nodded toward the row of staff lined up against the far wall. "I expect you'll make tomorrow just as amazing." He turned back to Tasha and her guests. "And I want to welcome you all to Sapphire Cay on behalf of Natasha and Liam." He glanced down at his sister, relieved to find a smile on her face and Liam's arm around her shoulder. "Obviously, we've a few guests missing right now so I'll save my best lines for tomorrow for maximum embarrassment on Tasha's part." He grinned as Liam laughed. Turning to Tasha, he raised his glass. "I just want to wish you all the best for tomorrow. I know Mom and Dad would have been incredibly proud." He smiled and held his glass out toward Tasha. "To Tasha and Liam."

"To Tasha and Liam," the guests repeated.

Lucas smiled as he sipped his drink.

Tasha wrapped her hand around his and pulled him down into his seat. "Thank you," she said, and there was a twinge in Lucas's chest when he found tears glazing her hazel eyes. Had it really been ten years? He remembered the day like it was yesterday—Officers Jenkins and Tabor standing in his parents' living room with their hats in their hands and offering their condolences. Tenderly, he cupped her cheek and then slid his hand through her blonde hair so like his own.

Leaning over, he kissed her cheek. "Don't go ruining your makeup," he whispered. Tasha laughed and his heart swelled with pride and warmth. They hadn't done so bad since their parents had been cruelly taken from them. Tasha was a beautiful and successful young woman, and she was going to be an equally amazing wife and mother.

Whether he was part of her life or not, she was going to do just fine.

"Ladies and gentlemen, would you like to move the party outside to the pool area. We have much to set up for tomorrow," the wedding coordinator announced with his clipped British accent. The suited and booted cliché-gay was a little too sure of himself for Lucas's liking, but he was to the point and beyond efficient, if not slightly regimental. Seriously, at one point, Lucas felt like they were preparing for battle, not a wedding. "Help yourselves to another glass of champagne as you leave. The bar will open shortly."

"Isn't Edward amazing? He's gay you know. Well, I don't know for sure but he probably is," Kate slurred from Lucas's right. She leaned forward and Lucas feared he was about to see far more of Kate than he really needed to. "It's going to be so beautiful tomorrow. Do you think he has a boyfriend? I mean, you could totally be his boyfriend, right?" At that point her husband wrapped his hands around her wrist and gently guided her back to him. Lucas couldn't have been more grateful. Sure the wedding coordinator was kind of cute in a straight-laced, up-his-own-ass kind of way, but totally not his type and definitely not what he needed right now. Edward edged towards being a bit too obvious and colorful for Lucas to feel entirely comfortable. What he had to do now was high-maintenance enough without having a partner like that demanding his time and energy.

Lucas rested his elbow on the table and watched the flurry of movement as everyone excitedly followed his sister and her fiancé to the exit. He smiled as he watched his sister's friend, Kate, being guided around the furniture and toward the door. He couldn't remember seeing her without a drink all evening, and it seemed alcohol and the heat had finally taken their toll. Downing what was left of his glass of champagne, Lucas got to his feet. Kate wasn't the only one flagging. The day had been a continuous parade of 'doing'—the flight, the boat ride, checking in, unpacking, showering, changing, the rehearsal, drinks, and the meal. And somehow, he'd managed to grab an hour to skim through the first several pages of the contract, and already he regretted it. Patterson had certainly screwed the pooch this time. Municipal wouldn't be happy with the offer he'd made, and it was going to take some serious backpedaling to get this thing fixed and calm the waters. What Patterson had done was beneficial to workers and owners alike but it cut Municipal's percentage to under six percent. To Lucas's mind this was a good deal and the kind of thing he wished Municipal negotiated every time. Municipal knew Lucas was good. Lucas knew he was good. But this good? Somehow, he needed to redo the contract, raise Municipal's percentage, and all the while not screw over staff and owners of the respective companies, or, indeed, Patterson.

With a sigh, Lucas slid his glass onto the table and made his way outside. He closed his eyes as he was greeted with cooler air mixed in with the humidity. Thank God. Since arriving on the island he'd had a constant layer of sticky sweat between him and his clothes. Even in the lightweight chinos and casual, short-sleeved shirt, Lucas had felt overwhelmed with the heat. But finally the promised cooler evening had arrived, and it was very much appreciated.

A high-pitched squeal suddenly erupted from among the guests and Lucas opened his eyes in time to see Kate's husband lift her from the ground. She squealed and kicked her legs, losing one of her expensive sandals as she was tossed through the air and came down with an almighty splash in the pool. What was it about alcohol that had grown adults behaving like children? He couldn't help but laugh as Kate stood up in the pool and smacked her hands against the surface of the water. She looked like she was about to have a full-on tantrum. Angrily, she pulled her wet hair back from her face and screeched at her husband, claiming he was a dead man. Lucas smiled as the guests burst into laughter and the one sober and sensible head of the group, Vanessa, Liam's mom, began shooing them from the poolside. His smile turned to a smirk as Vanessa held out her hands to Kate. A risky move for the prim and proper sixty-year-old. He half expected—and in a small way kind of wanted—Kate to grab the woman's hand and pull Vanessa in alongside her. Fortunately, that didn't happen, and instead, Kate emerged from the water drenched and dripping and glaring at her husband. Lucas should really have listened to his name when Kate introduced them. He would like to shake that man's hand and applaud his bravery, because from the look on Kate's face, he was totally in for it when she got him alone.

Leaving the rest of the guests to their games, Lucas wandered idly across the decking and down the single step to the small bar. Wooden in structure, it mixed the modern, classy smooth edges and neutral colors of a city cocktail bar with a whimsical tropical feel with its grass roof, lanterns, and chains of fake orchids and various other brightly colored flowers. He stopped as he reached the bar and rested against the solid edge. Leaning his head to one side, he admired the view. Now this was something he could appreciate. He stared at the ass of the figure behind the counter. The bartender was distracted, crouched down in front of one of the coolers and arranging bottles of drink so their labels faced outward. Lucas slid onto one of the barstools and continued to watch. The bartender was wearing tight, black jeans that accentuated the curve of his ass, and a sliver of tanned skin was on show as he bent over and his white shirt rode up his back.

"What can I get ya?" sexy-assed bartender said as he got to his feet.

Lucas sat up straight, surprised the bartender knew he was there. "Erm…" What the hell did he want? The bartender turned around and Lucas was pretty sure his jaw hit the bar as he stared up at the same man who had brought them over on the boat. "Oh, hi," he managed and quickly averted his gaze and glanced over to where Tasha and Liam were locked in an embrace. Their profiles were set against a net of twinkling fairy lights and he couldn't remember them ever looking as in love and happy as they did right now.

"Brother of the bride, right?" the barman asked.

Lucas nodded, adjusting his position to sit more comfortably. "Captain Dylan," he said and flashed a smile.

"Just Dylan." The captain, *Dylan*, looked past Lucas at the rest of the wedding party. "They look like they're having fun."

Lucas turned on his stool and looked across the group of guests. Kate seemed oblivious to the fact she looked like a half-drowned rat as she held a glass of champagne in her hand and was deep in conversation with Vanessa. Kate's husband was keeping his distance and sharing a joke with Tasha's remaining guests.

"So, what can I get for you?" Dylan asked again and rested his hands on the bar as he waited.

On the bar was a cocktail list. Picking it up, Lucas eyed the various concoctions. "What would you suggest?" he said and laid the menu out flat.

Dylan scanned the list. "Sex on the Beach is quite popular." He gave a mischievous grin, as his eyes briefly met Lucas's. Their rich ocean blue was more beautiful than anything Lucas had imagined lay behind the shades Dylan wore on the boat.

Lucas drew his lower lip between his teeth. "I'm not crazy about sand," he said suggestively and then focused on the cocktails. "I'll have an Apple Mojito. Thanks." He closed the menu and pushed it to one side.

"Coming right up." Dylan turned and searched for the ingredients to put together the Mojito—rum, apple liqueur, soda water, lime, syrup, crushed ice, and mint leaves.

Lucas watched the flick of Dylan's wrist as he muddled the lime and syrup with the mint leaves. "So, are you a boat-guy moonlighting as a cocktail-guy or the other way around?" he asked. He wasn't sure which to bet on. Dylan was lean and tanned, stubble covered his jaw, and Lucas could see him halfway to crusty old seadog already. And yet with the tight jeans and the white, open-collar shirt, his hair swept back from his face, and the finesse with which he was pouring and mixing, Dylan definitely had the exotic bartender feel to him.

Pouring the drink over ice, Dylan then finished the glass with a slice of lime, fresh mint leaves, and a straw. "What would you say if I said neither and both?" Dylan accompanied his mysterious answer with a grin. Rolling up his sleeves, he slid the glass toward Lucas.

The drink looked good, as did the man who made it. Lucas's gaze drifted from the drink to the inside of Dylan's wrist and the tattoo that was now visible. He stared at the outline of a spiraling sun, made up of a large circle with equally spaced curved rays around its circumference. It was filled in a mixture of yellow and orange and words were written beneath it in a script Lucas couldn't read from where he was.

"Is that for me?" Tasha chimed in as she stumbled up against him and flopped across his lap.

"No," he said and sucked on his straw. The rum and apple taste was refreshing, and he had to stop himself before he finished the drink too quickly. "How the hell are you going to get up in the morning?" Was he supposed to look after her now that Kate was pool-soaked and definitely not sober?

"I'm fine. Stop being a party pooper and have some fun."

Lucas rolled his eyes upward and stared at the night sky. It was clear and the stars shone brightly.

"I mean it," Tasha continued. "It's a vacation. I don't want you working all week or next week. You could do with getting a tan and drinking cocktails out of coconuts."

She stopped and looked up at Dylan. "You do have cocktails in coconuts, right?"

"They can certainly be arranged," Dylan said with a smile.

"See?" She stood up and wrapped her arm around Lucas's shoulder. "Please, for me and for you, no work while you're here." Tasha put on a firm look. "I mean it. I worry about you. I don't want to lose you." Unspoken was Alan and everything he had left behind.

"Tasha!" Thank God. They both turned to where Liam was motioning for her to join him. Soon they would go to their separate rooms and Liam was evidently keen to spend as much time with her as possible before that happened.

"Promise," Tasha said.

Lucas debated what to do. "Promise," he lied. He watched as Tasha made her way unsteadily in three-inch heels back to her husband-to-be.

"Are you okay?" Dylan asked, and Lucas tiredly pinched the bridge of his nose. "Your sister seems a real sweet girl."

"She is," Lucas said and rested his arms on the bar. He thoughtfully looked up at Dylan. *Boat-guy or cocktail-guy?* "Do you ever feel like you should be somewhere else, doing something else?"

Dylan met Lucas's eyes and nodded. "Of course." He smiled and leaned on the bar opposite Lucas. "It's why I'm not the sole captain of that boat or the bartender mixing cocktails past the end of next month."

Narrowing his eyes, Lucas needed to ask. "Why?"

"I've never subscribed to the whole settling for just one thing. There are a million and one places to visit, people to talk to, and jobs to have." Despite saying this, Dylan had a thoughtful expression on his face. If he had made that statement with a grin then Lucas may well have left it but something about Dylan's demeanor made him want to carry on this thread of conversation.

"But aren't some things worth settling for?" Lucas asked. Because of his job, Tasha had never wanted for anything. That was a good thing. Right?

"Sure, I guess," Dylan said and leaned back as Kate's husband joined Lucas at the bar. He glanced at Lucas and smiled. "If you settle for the right reasons."

Not knowing what else to say, Lucas nodded his reply, and then taking his drink, he left his seat and walked past the hut, down onto the beach. Awkwardly and one-handed, making sure not to spill the drink, he removed shoes and socks and then left them in a small pile as he wandered down towards the gently rolling waves. The night was warm and there was a faint breeze that ruffled through his hair and brought with it the scent of the sea.

He reached the water and immediately took a step into the cool sea, not really caring that the bottoms of his pants were getting wet. He'd packed shorts and cutoffs for after the wedding, getting this spare pair of dress pants wet meant he was more likely to wear the shorts. The only way to make sure he lived a little.

His mind went from work to Alan to his health and inevitably settled on Tasha.

Her meeting Liam, a man who could provide for her as well as Lucas had done, was the other part to this complicated jigsaw Lucas called life. In his opinion, no man would ever be good enough for his sister, but Liam came damn close. He was a solid, steady man with a passionate soul, and Tasha and he were perfect for each other. She had wanted Lucas to leave Municipal as soon as she heard Alan had died. She worried about Lucas as much as he worried about her.

"And you think the stress won't kill you as well?" she said with passion. "You're thirty-two years old yet you walk around exhausted and gray. I never see you, and I worry."

"It isn't like that," he defended. "I'm younger than Alan and I know my limits—"

"So did Alan."

He had no response to that one really. He could lie to everyone as much as he wanted, but he couldn't lie to himself anymore. Instead, he focused on the why of working as opposed to the actual doing.

"I work so I have something for the future."

"You've said that before, Luc, and I'm the only one that can say this to you. Alan had a solid future—a pension, a family."

Sighing, he kicked at a small pile of sand on the edge of the water as he walked out of the water and back onto the beach. He glanced up at the beautiful hotel, lit with a thousand low lamps that cast a glow out into the surrounding darkness. The air was still humid, but there was a breeze coming in off the sea and the whoosh of the waves lulled him out of his introspection. He had to draw a line under his working life and decide what he was going to do now; it was the only way to move forward. Folding his legs under him, he sat cross-legged on the soft sand and looked out at the blackness of dark sky and iron sea.

Was it the best thing for him to take up a new role on the fourth of next month? Was it worth losing his health and living on pills for the rest of his life? Would he be able to leave Municipal once the bonus for this last job was paid? Or should he change the direction of his whole life? He bet Alan would have wanted another chance to make these kinds of decisions.

Chapter Three

HOW LONG HE SAT THERE HE DIDN'T KNOW. THE SOUNDS of partying sometimes reached him—laughter and the odd splash—but down here on the beach he had time to think. His watch was in his room and he didn't have the energy to wrestle his cell from his back pocket. Completely cut off from the passage of time, he could really lose himself in the peace of the ocean.

"Do you mind company?"

Lucas looked up and blinked at the bar-guy-slash-captain, Dylan, who was standing way tall and looking down at him with a smile.

"It's a free beach," Lucas said. He pushed down the instinctive thrill of pleasure that tall, dark, and sexy-rough wanted to sit next to him. Then just as quickly, he wondered why Dylan was here at all. "Aren't you working?"

"Everyone's in bed, it's nearly midnight."

"It is?" Lucas shook his head. Hours had passed as he

watched the waves reach shore and then recede into the darkness.

"I brought you another Apple Mojito," Dylan said. Passing the drink down and carefully balancing his own bottled beer, Dylan made himself comfortable at Lucas's side. "You look like a man who needs a drink."

"And how is that?"

"All starry-eyed into the distance." Dylan shook his free hand in a loose approximation of pointing out there into the dark. "Clearly, you have big thoughts."

"It's a big day tomorrow. I'm giving away my only family."

"To be fair, Liam seems like a nice guy."

Lucas cast a look sideways at Dylan. He was a staff member. Should he really be down here making personal comments to guests?

"He is. A very nice man," Lucas finally answered.

"Can I ask you a question?"

"Uh huh?"

"You're gay, right? I overheard it on the boat."

Lucas turned to look at Dylan, but his companion's gaze was fixed firmly out to sea as he asked the question.

"I don't think that's an appropriate—" he started, but then stopped abruptly. Who was he kidding? When Dylan turned to face him with that open expression and a faint smile on his lips, Lucas could only really say one thing. After all, Dylan had heard what Kate had said, and had probably noticed him staring at his ass when he was organizing bottles in the fridge. "Yes."

"Don't you want to know why I asked you?" Dylan's voice was soft and invited confidence.

"Tell me," Lucas said.

"I kind of wanted to ruffle your feathers a bit. Are you out?"

"To family—what there is of it—and to friends."

"Oh." Dylan's voice held a note of puzzlement. "You were so distracted, first on the boat with that redhead, and then at the bar. Thought maybe you were still in the closet and it was a battle with not wanting people to know."

Lucas huffed a laugh at Dylan's comment. If only his problems were something that well defined. He didn't care who knew he was gay. He was happy in his own skin, and so far prejudice and hate hadn't really touched him. Even Oscar, his boss, knew, and although he had commented on the fact, it didn't seem to make Lucas a lesser manager in his eyes.

"I just have a lot on my mind."

"Your sister?"

"Tasha? No, she's golden. She's with a man who loves her and who will treat her right. Liam is one of the good guys."

Dylan frowned and took a swallow of his beer. "So, you're happy in your own skin and your close family has a good life. Why do you look so sad?"

"Is this a bartender thing? Where you ask random shit like that and I sit and tell you all my problems?" Lucas laughed. "Sad? I don't feel sad," he lied through his teeth. His nerves were too raw to talk about Alan or about the decisions he faced about his future. Neither subject was what he wanted to talk about to the first available person who trapped him in a dark space and beguiled him with soft emotional questions. Not that he was exactly trapped.

"Okay," Dylan said softly.

"Look. My gaydar is for shit. I'm guessing since it's probably not hotel policy to ask guests directly about their sexual orientation that you are gay as well? Is it so you can flirt and get better tips from me and we'll 'all be gay together'?" He said the last bracketed with air quotes and inserted sarcasm into his tone. "Or are you going to give me some shit about how you're straight but sexuality is a fluid thing and you're cool with it, blah blah?"

"Hostile much?" Dylan joked. He cracked a smile—and that smile was incendiary. It sent blood to Lucas's dick faster than you could say 'sex'. Wriggling a bit without making it too obvious, he focused on the smile. Dylan was talking. "Yes, I'm gay, and no, I'm not flirting with you because I want better tips. I'm doing it because I thought a bit of harmless playing might make the next two weeks a little happier for you."

"Oh." Now he was really at a loss for words. He considered his response, but then his cell vibrated in his pocket and he reacted instantly by pulling it out to check the screen. Oscar. Tension and familiar stress prickled at the base of his neck as his shoulders tightened. Why the hell was Oscar calling this late?

"Excuse me a minute," he said politely. He had no choice. If he didn't speak now then what the hell would he find on his voicemail in ten minutes? At least talking to Oscar directly meant he had a chance in hell of managing the whole clusterfuck that was his work life at the moment. "I have to take this."

DYLAN WASN'T REALLY TRYING TO LISTEN. OF COURSE, HE wasn't really trying to ignore what Lucas was talking about either. This man sat here on beautiful Sapphire Cay was using terminology that would best be on the financial pages of the *New York Times*. Throwing words around like they meant something special, Lucas's voice escalated from calm to brusque to subservient to deceitful. Dylan had seen this type of man before—a big-shot businessman lost in the world of high-rise city blocks and power lunches.

Definitely not my kind of lover.

But there was the air of sadness about Lucas and it alternately intrigued and worried him. The contrast of lost-boy sadness and snarky humor now to the clipped business tone on the boat was such a direct contradiction. Those differences were like a flame and he was the freaking moth drawn to it.

The discussion seemed to be heating up and he decided it was probably best to withdraw politely. With a sketched salute of his hand, he clambered to stand and then made his way up the beach. No sense in him being there really if this was an important call. He knew that from experience.

Even in hospital, his dad would be lost to him as soon as the phone rang. Dylan Gray, Senior was an exec—respected and trusted in his field of whatever the hell it was, futures or something equally as nonsensical.

No sense in flirting with Lucas for a holiday fling then, if all that was left for Dylan was a few scraps of time. Shame. Lucas was hot and lithe—just what he liked in his men. Also, it had been a long time since he'd had fun that didn't just involve his right hand and his imagination. He screwed up his face in thought—it had to be going on a year now. Never mind. He was off to LA at the end of next month for another bartending gig. The peak of the hurricane season was only a month or two away and he always followed the sun. That was his mantra in life. A few months there and then maybe he'd go look up friends in San Diego, or even travel down to Texas. It didn't matter what the work was as long as he stayed brown and healthy and paid his way.

He stopped just short of the tree line to the far left of the hotel and turned around to check on Lucas. The man was standing, call finished, with his arms wrapped around his chest and his head bowed. There was real defeat in his posture. Leaning back against the smooth bark of the nearest palm tree, Dylan remained watchful. Something wasn't right there. Whatever was happening was a heavy burden on Lucas's back. As if sensing his gaze, Lucas turned to look directly where he was standing and then began to walk toward him.

"Sorry," he said when he was finally standing in front of Dylan.

"It's fine. I know what it's like."

"They won't leave me alone." Frustration snapped in his voice. This was a different reaction than what Dylan expected. Even on their one aborted post-cancer vacation, his dad held onto that connection to his office with a tenacious grip. Didn't matter where they were, he was always in touch with anything that could go wrong back home. After losing his wife when she gave birth to their only child and then the stress of Dylan getting sick with cancer, his dad had clung to work like a drowning man held onto a life preserver.

Lucas closed his eyes briefly. Evidently he was clearing his thoughts of work and jumping back to where they were before. Then he looked up at Dylan with such incredible sadness in his eyes that Dylan could no more ignore than he could ignore a puppy in the rain. Reaching the short distance, he pulled Lucas towards him and settled him close. At first Lucas resisted the pull, but when it became clear Dylan wasn't letting go, he just gave in. He crumbled. Completely and utterly.

"Do you want to talk about it?" he asked. Lucas shook his head mutely. Dylan's nature couldn't let Lucas stay so tense and very slowly, he began a gentle motion of pressing and releasing his hands on Lucas's back, sliding them from neck to the base of his spine and back again. Lucas made a small sound of encouragement that slipped out on a sigh. Lucas was so tense, but slowly as Dylan massaged and pressed, all the while holding Lucas's weight against him, he started to relax.

Lucas pressed his face into Dylan's neck and rested, still for a few seconds. Then he began to kiss where his lips touched bare skin and Dylan was hard in seconds. The feel of this man against him, pliant and quiet in the darkness, was intoxicating. When the kissing moved up to his chin and trailed to his mouth, Dylan shifted a little so that they were level, and finally he was able to relieve some of the pressure in his dick by pushing it firmly against Lucas. Their lips met in a kiss that was gentle. Tilting his head, he let Lucas control the kiss until finally the slide of tongues gave him his first taste of Lucas and Apple Mojito. They stood for a long time, the lazy slip of slick lips and the press of their bodies creating a heat that Dylan found he craved.

Instead, Lucas pulled back and Dylan let him loose. He concentrated on the breathing that caused Lucas's chest to rise and fall, then looked up slowly and saw Lucas's teeth worrying his lower lip. Leaning forward, he gently kissed that small area.

"Don't do that. Your sister won't like it if her photos are ruined."

Lucas looked down at himself and then back up. That familiar disappointment was back in his eyes. What did he see when he looked down at himself like that? Dylan bet it wasn't a hot body and sex that leaked from every pore. In fact, Dylan would put money on the fact that Lucas didn't see himself as either of those things.

"I'll see you in the morning," Lucas finally said. Reaching up, he carded a hand into Dylan's hair and smiled. "Thank you," he whispered. With that, he turned on his heel and headed back to the hotel. Dylan watched as Lucas picked up his shoes and then waited until there was no sign of Lucas, or indeed anyone else. Resting his head back against the tree, he inhaled the warm, salty air and smiled.

He wasn't sure what it was about Lucas that had him standing here like an idiot, smiling. There was simply something in Lucas's eyes that spoke of sadness and fear. Not the first emotions he thought he would see in the brother of a bride on this island.

Pushing himself away from the trunk, he sauntered away from the hotel and over to the small, cabin-like place he called home when he was here. Little more than four walls, a bed, and a small kitchen, it was perfect for him. He was hardly ever inside anyway. There was a message on his cell phone. The old Nokia still lived and it was the number that only his dad knew. There was a simple message telling him that his signature was needed on some paperwork. No questions about how he was or what he was doing, just that they needed to arrange a meet with a legal representative.

Why did he even keep the damn thing charged and registered? When every single text or message would drag him back to a life he didn't want? Carefully, he unplugged the cell from the charger and just as deliberately placed it back in the top drawer of his unit. Clearly, the signature wasn't life or death else his dad would have sent someone to find him. It could wait.

Grabbing a blanket, he went back out onto the sand and lay flat on his back, looking up at the stars. Lucas intrigued him and spending time thinking about him meant, for one moment, he didn't have to focus on the man who gave him life only to spend the next nearly twenty-five years trying to suck that life back out of him and everything around him.

Lucas with the short spiky blond hair and with beautiful amber-flecked hazel eyes that held sadness and secrets. Dylan would give anything to bury his hands in Lucas's hair and chase some of that sadness in his expression away.

Why? He wasn't entirely sure. But he was utterly determined to try.

Chapter Four

"OH, TASH. YOU LOOK AMAZING." LUCAS'S HEART swelled with pride as he gazed at his sister. She was absolutely stunning and he wasn't sure he had the words to truly describe how proud he was. He really couldn't remember a time when she'd looked more beautiful than she did now. Her dress was simple but elegant: floor-length and made from silk, with a low neckline and diamante detail at her waist. It suited her figure beautifully and shimmered in the sunlight streaming through the bedroom window. The front section of her hair had been pinned back from her face, set off with a silver spiral hairclip, and then left to fall in soft curls around her neck and shoulders. Everything was perfect.

"It's okay?" Tasha asked shyly and gave a delicate twirl before stopping and rocking on the heels of her silver sandals. Her hands tightened around her white orchid bouquet as she exhaled loudly and met his eyes. She shouldn't be nervous.

Lucas stepped forward and wrapped his hands around

hers. She was trembling. "It's more than okay." He smiled and carefully pulled her into a half hug. The last thing he wanted was to be in trouble for crushing her bouquet or his matching buttonhole. "Liam's a lucky guy," he said in a low voice and affectionately kissed her cheek before releasing her.

Tasha smiled brightly and relaxed her shoulders. "Thank you. And thank you for everything else."

"Everything else?" Lucas looked curiously at his sister. Apart from writing a check and getting on a plane, he'd had very little input in the whole affair. Tasha stared up at him and he took the moment to look over her immaculate makeup. Kate had done a great job. Tasha's hazel eyes were framed with blue-tinted eyeliner and a dusting of silver eye shadow, blush added definition to her cheekbones, and her lips were coated in a pale peach gloss. His gaze returned to her eyes and sadness quickly enveloped him. There were tears in Tasha's eyes. "Hey. What's wrong?" he asked and soothingly rubbed the tops of her arms.

Shaking her head, Tasha ran her thumb beneath her eyes trying to stave off the tears. "Nothing." She fanned her face with her hand and pressed her lips together in a quivering pout. "Just…" Blowing out a breath, she looked at Lucas. She seemed overwhelmed. "I'm just being silly." She met Lucas's eyes and gave a sad smile. "I don't know what I'd do without you."

"Now you *are* being silly," Lucas gently chided. She was marrying a good man and they were going to start a family of their own. She deserved to be happy and surrounded by people who loved her.

Tasha nodded. "Maybe." She narrowed her eyes as she looked at him. Something still bothered her. "You'd tell me if there was something wrong, wouldn't you?"

"Of course," Lucas said quickly. She shouldn't be thinking about him today. "I'm fine. Really. I'm not Alan." He did his best to reassure her, though it did little to reassure himself. His friend was again at the forefront of his mind. He wasn't like Alan, he told himself. He really wasn't. Things had been caught early. Yes, what happened to Alan was sad. Hell, he had buried himself in grief and paperwork for days after it happened. But he also knew he had to use it. Use all that anger and misery and have the balls to walk away. He planned to hang onto life with both hands and stick around a hell of a lot longer yet. He was only just in his thirties. The prime of his life, right? He shouldn't have an ulcer or soaring blood pressure and migraines. He should be doing stuff. What, he wasn't entirely sure, but he knew he shouldn't be digging himself an early grave. He wanted to live and enjoy life again. He wanted to see Tasha bloom, start a family, and make a life for herself.

"Now stop it," he said firmly. "This is your day, Tash." There was a twinge in his chest as he met her eyes that he could only describe as guilt. He hated lying to her. But what the hell else was he supposed to say?

It was better this way, at least for now. She'd only be fussing over him and this vacation wasn't about him. He wanted to forget about the doctor and the pills and the future appointments, about Municipal and the fucking contract. All he wanted to do was see his sister enjoy herself and marry the man she loved. Surely he must have earned that right? Just one perfect fucking day? Tasha looked at him and he knew she didn't believe him, not completely. He was good at his job and ninety percent of the time could talk a winning game, but with her? He wouldn't say it was a one hundred percent failure rate, but it was pretty damn close. She very often spotted his lies before he even had chance to tell them.

Thankfully, Tasha didn't get chance to call him on it as there was a knock on the door.

"Everything okay?" Kate asked as she stepped into the room. She smiled sweetly as she rested a hand on her hip and her cerulean blue chiffon cocktail dress rose to above her knee. Her red hair was swept back from her face in a French braid and a pale purple flower was fastened above her ear, matching the accent color of her and Tasha's bouquets. It was quite the transformation from the drunken mother of two whose company he'd had the pleasure of last night. "Photographer's here."

Tasha nodded and gently pushed at her hair, checking on the volume of her curls. "Did everybody else make it over okay?" The last of the guests had been due to arrive that morning. It brought the bridal party up to a total of fifteen.

"Yes," Kate said with certainty. "Everybody's checked in, dressed, and have already taken their seats."

Turning to Lucas, Tasha took his hand in hers. She squeezed it tightly as she looked to him for support. She looked beautiful.

"You ready?" Lucas asked.

Tasha simply gave another nod.

"I'll send him in," Kate said of the photographer before ducking out of the room.

Lucas quickly checked himself out in the long mirror on the closet door. Was it evening yet? He could already feel sweat collecting at the base of his spine beneath the pale blue shirt and light gray suit jacket. It was a beach wedding. Couldn't they all just wear shorts and T-shirts? With a sigh, he combed his fingers through his hair. Maybe after today he could spend some time on the beach. He hadn't seen it before, despite Tasha's observations, but he really did look tired and gray.

"Good mornin', folks. How are we all doin'?"

Lucas turned around as he heard the familiar southern-warm voice. He raised an eyebrow as he came face to face with Dylan. *You have got to be kidding me?!*

"You look gorgeous, honey," Dylan said and leaned in to kiss Tasha. "And you're not so bad either," he said to Lucas. Dylan gave a friendly nod in his direction and flashed a wide smile. What was Dylan doing here? Didn't he have a boat to drive or a bar to run or gay guys to sniff out?

"You're the photographer?" Lucas asked drily and folded his arms across his chest. He didn't mean to come across as hostile, but he suddenly felt incredibly uncomfortable and embarrassed. Dylan just kept turning up like the proverbial penny. He pursed his lips as he looked Dylan up and down. Jealousy reared inside him as he eyed Dylan's board shorts and open-neck white cotton shirt. He really couldn't wait to get out of his suit. His eyes drifted upward. Okay, so maybe Dylan wasn't like the 'penny', because the 'penny' was a bad thing and Dylan certainly wasn't that. In fact, he was the complete opposite. Yes, Lucas was utterly embarrassed about last night. Hell, he'd halfway thrown himself on Dylan—at least that's how he imagined it had looked—and the thought left him mortified. The memory of ocean, sand, and the solid, grounded feel of Dylan holding him made his chest tighten and his heart ache. He had needed that. He had needed Dylan. Everything else had seemed so complicated and all he felt was lost in a swirl of despair. Dylan had been there and the taste of his sun-warmed skin and lips had been incredible. Dylan had tasted like the ocean, like freedom, and it had been easy and safe. If only everything could be like that.

"A man of many talents," Tasha said to Dylan, pulling Lucas from his thoughts.

Lucas met Dylan's curious eyes. Crap, had he been staring all this time? Clearing his throat, he averted his eyes, only to find Tasha's. She gave him a mischievous look. What had she seen? What did she think she knew? By the curl of her lips, she was already way ahead of herself and obviously completely wrong. He'd deny anything and everything later.

"Indeed I am," Dylan said playfully and looked around the room. "Anything in particular you'd like? Or would you like me to direct you?"

"We're happy to follow your lead. Aren't we, Luc?"

Lucas kept his eyes on Tasha and gave a short nod. "Sure. Whatever you think." He pulled at his collar.

Dylan smiled. "Okay. Let's start by the bed."

Shouldn't the resort be providing a real photographer? Isn't that what he paid for? Dylan did look to have all the right equipment and the camera he was holding looked expensive. He waited until Dylan took the first few and then demanded to see them. They were good. Dylan was good. Finally, he relaxed.

DYLAN NARROWED HIS EYES AND TOOK A SERIES OF SHOTS.

"Lucas, if you turn a little more to the right. Tasha, lower your flowers." Lowering the digital camera, he checked through the last few images. "Okay. I think we're done." He briefly locked eyes with Lucas. Lucas looked uncomfortable and screamed 'awkward', but Dylan couldn't figure out if it was the camera or if it was him being there that was the problem. Okay, so last night had been a little strange, but it wasn't like anything had happened between them. Not really. Normally, Dylan wouldn't care and would rack it up to misjudgment and move on, but there was just something about Lucas that had him interested—Lucas with his sad eyes and full, kissable lips.

"Can I have a quick word?" Lucas asked.

Dylan looked up from his camera. The girls were busying themselves with last minute touch-ups to their hair and makeup, leaving Lucas free to talk. "Sure," he said and let Lucas guide him out of the suite. "Everything okay?"

Lucas hesitated and leaned against the wall beside the door. There it was again. A dense, poignant air hung around Lucas and Dylan just wanted to reach out and shake him free. If ever he had seen someone more in need of a vacation, he couldn't remember, and it just sealed the urge he had to help Lucas have a good time while he was here at Sapphire Cay. What could be more fun and relaxing than a fling in the sun?

"So, you take photos?" he finally said and met Dylan's eyes.

Dylan pursed his lips. He doubted this was really what Lucas wanted to talk about, but if it was all he was going to get, he could work with that. "You don't need to worry. I can take a decent picture." He grinned. To be honest, the camera did most of the hard work. Auto-focus was his friend. "I won't let Natasha down."

Dylan understood why Lucas might be concerned. It was the most important day in his sister's life—or at least one of them. And to many people, photographs built up the most important memories of big events. But Lucas shouldn't worry. Dylan could use a camera; he could do plenty of other things too, and though he didn't want to sound like an egotistical dick, he had to confess he was good at pretty much everything he tried his hand at. Okay, so maybe not the pottery wheel. That had been a total disaster. It was not as easy as Moore and Swayze had made it look. He'd enjoyed the challenge though. And that was what it was all about. Variety, challenge, and always moving forward kept him happy.

Lucas appeared to relax a little and gave a slow nod. "Thanks. It means a lot."

"Hey, it's all cool. Antoine wouldn't give me the gig if he didn't trust me."

Antoine Durand and his wife, Jeanie, now in their late sixties, had managed the hotel at Sapphire Cay for almost thirty years. They had spent most of their lives transforming the island into what Dylan now considered perfection. It was the reason he kept coming back here. In some ways it probably went against what he believed in. For years, he'd stuck to the idea of following the sun and never looking back. But the earth was a sphere, and eventually, no matter what, he'd end up back where he started. And there was no better place to come back to time and time again. The people were amazing and the setting was just so idyllic, and he felt a peace here he just couldn't imagine finding anyplace else. No matter how far he travelled, how many people he met, and how many lovers' arms he melted into, nothing felt as much like home as the Cay. The couple were always good to him, and with their children all grown up and off doing their own thing, Dylan figured he kind of filled a space for them. Hell, sometimes it was a space he needed to fill. Those occasions when he found he missed playing the role of a son.

He realized Lucas was looking at him, and suddenly it was Dylan's turn to feel awkward. He had totally drifted off. "I promise, okay?" He smiled reassuringly as he patted his camera. "I should probably go and take some of the groom and guests and leave you to finish getting ready." He turned, ready to make his exit, but was surprised when Lucas touched his shoulder, stopping him.

"About last night," Lucas started. He wore a frown and seemed conflicted as he spoke. "I just want to apologize."

Dylan shrugged. "Nothing to apologize for." There wasn't. Sure, Lucas's lost-puppy routine had Dylan drawn like a kid to candy, but it wasn't anything Lucas needed to excuse. That was all Dylan and his slightly skewed preferences. Men with issues just brought out his desire to solve and help.

Lucas's eyes darkened. "I don't usually…" He held his hands out and motioned toward Dylan. "I don't usually do this kind of thing," he finally finished.

This kind of thing? When had they made it a thing? Laughing, Dylan shook his head. "It was just a kiss." He looked into Lucas's eyes and was surprised to find something that looked like disappointment. Was Lucas not trying to dismiss last night as a mistake and moment of insanity? "A very nice kiss," he added with a smile.

Closing his eyes, Lucas exhaled a heavy breath. There were plenty of other things going on today. It was a kiss. People kissed all the time. It was a thing people did. Dylan looked Lucas up and down and smiled. And if Lucas would, say, want to kiss again, Dylan wouldn't object.

"I should go," Dylan decided, disturbing Lucas from the quiet moment he was having. Maybe later he could figure out what it was that had Lucas all twisted around—and why the hell he cared so damn much.

"Yeah," Lucas said and opened his eyes. He looked like he wanted to say more, but instead began to worry his lower lip.

He probably shouldn't have, but Dylan slowly raised a hand and gently pressed his finger to Lucas's mouth. "Hey, remember what I said about ruining the photos?" he said warmly before pulling back his hand. Lucas's mouth was soft and inviting. He smiled as Lucas laughed. The sound went straight to his dick and he couldn't help but stare as Lucas's features softened and the laugh creased the corners of Lucas's eyes and dimpled his cheeks. It was true, laughter was like medicine. "I better go," he said again, trying to ignore the growing urge to just pull the man into a hug and kiss him senseless.

"Maybe I could buy you a drink later?" Lucas said quickly. "I mean, if you're not working, or after or something?"

Dylan smirked. "You know the drinks are free, right?" The wedding package was priced to cover the cost of the bar, the staff, and the copious amounts of alcohol that would no doubt be drunk during the day.

Lucas looked embarrassed as he examined his feet, and Dylan thought it was one of the sweetest things he'd ever seen. It was good Lucas was making the next move.

"But sure," Dylan said. "After I'm finished with my photographer duties, a drink sounds great." He met Lucas's eyes and admired the bright flash of amber. The space between them suddenly didn't feel so great. Was this Lucas's way of letting him in? Dylan continued in his appraisal of Lucas. The man was hot and Dylan was now even more convinced than ever Lucas didn't realize just how desirable he was—full lips, kind eyes, and a body Dylan would enjoy exploring. Lucas was intriguing and a damn distraction. "Right, I really need to go." He gained his focus and smiled. There were photographs to take. He edged backward.

"So, later?" Lucas checked.

"Later." Dylan gave a brief wave as he left. Later sounded absolutely perfect.

Chapter Five

THE SUN HAD BEGUN ITS DESCENT AND THE RAW HEAT OF the day was lessening when Lucas stood at the edge of the beach with Tasha. She held onto his arm with a grip of iron. Trees hid them from the gathered friends and the hotel staff, and they stood there for a second. Lucas didn't push her to talk, and by the grin on her face, she wasn't having second thoughts.

"This is my last chance," she said. Her voice held laughter and not one iota of nerves.

I can do this. He could be calm and joke and laugh.

"We could still run away and steal a boat. It's not too late," Lucas joked. "I can't understand what you see if him. I mean, yeah, he's gorgeous, sexy, confident, rich, and loves you, but besides that..." He laughed along with Tasha as she leaned in close and he kissed her cheek.

"I love you, Luc," she said.

"I love you too, sis."

"Thank you. For standing in for dad. For being the person who looked after me."

"Tasha—"

"I mean it. You could have palmed me off with any one of a hundred different official people, but you didn't."

For a second, Lucas started to speak, but then he stopped. There weren't any words for this situation. Tears caught in his throat that their mom and dad weren't here. His sister had a new start. He was going to miss having a reason to be in her life. He wasn't so much doing the whole ceremonial giving away; he literally was handing her over to another man, trusting that Liam would look after Tasha.

"Wanna get married?" he finally said.

Smiling, she turned to face the short path to the beach, and drawing back her shoulders, she took the first step towards the rest of her life. Liam was waiting, dressed similarly to Lucas but with a purple accent in his shirt and buttonhole. All too soon they were there, and among the few close friends that Tasha had, she and Liam spoke their vows and promised each other forever. The official was sun-brown and young and for a millisecond Lucas wondered why it wasn't Dylan officiating here—after all, he did everything else. Casting a casual eye around the people here for the ceremony, he couldn't believe the sharp stab of disappointment that caught him by surprise. Stupid that after not even two days, just glimpsing Dylan —as captain, bartender, or photographer—made him so happy and flooded with possibilities. Where was Dylan now? Shouldn't he be taking photographs of the ceremony? Wait. There he was to the right of the ceremony, where Lucas couldn't see clearly. After a few shots, Dylan moved in among the gathered people, snapping some informal shots before waiting for the next part.

The ceremony finished with a long kiss and he laughed and clapped alongside everyone else as the bride and groom walked away from the ceremony and down to the shoreline where Dylan posed them and began shooting photos. Lucas imagined the beauty of the shots against the foam of the sea and the darkening blue of the sky. Hundreds of small lamps twinkled in trees, and for the first time he could really understand why Tasha wanted to get married here.

"Beautiful," Kate said. She was bright-eyed and her voice sounded a little choked. Pushed by some instinct to connect, he pulled Kate into a quick hug and then released her before she could grip him back. She didn't comment as she was whisked away by her husband, but that didn't stop the smile on her face as she looked back at him. He returned the smile and then turned to watch his sister—it was disconcerting to connect like that with anyone, let alone his sister's loud friend. Tasha and Liam were standing at the water's edge in each other's arms, but there was no sign of Dylan. Evidently, he had finished his work at that point, which, if Lucas remembered right, left only the first dance photos and a few as they gave speeches.

The reality of the speech he had to give only hit him when every eye turned to him expectantly and everyone held flutes of champagne.

"I had a long list of embarrassing stories to tell you all," he began. Tasha groaned and covered her eyes with her free hand. There was laughter as Liam kissed the hand away. This was a good start to the speech—people laughed

—and Lucas felt himself relax. "At the end of the day, though, Tash and I have been there for each other every single day and I couldn't have wished for a wiser, braver, and more beautiful sister." There was some oohing and aahing and Tasha smiled softly with tears glistening in her eyes.

"I know Mom and Dad would have been so proud of the woman their daughter has become. They would have been so pleased that Liam decided to visit the same bar as her for a night of debauchery." Again a few laughs. The standing joke was that both Liam and Tasha had gone out for nothing more than drinks and had ended up setting a second date, and then a third. "I felt like no man could love my sister as much as I do, but Liam proved me wrong. Please, raise your glasses and toast. To the bride and groom."

Everyone repeated the words and Lucas had to push down the emotion flooding him as Liam placed his champagne glass to one side, relieved Tasha of hers, and then bent Tasha back in an exaggerated Hollywood kiss.

Lucas may not have spent as much time with her as he should, but she had always been there, just forty minutes away. Now she wouldn't be just around the corner. Liam's company was opening a new office in Washington DC, and he and Tasha were moving pretty much straight after the wedding. She walked over to Lucas and pulled him into a close hug. There were no words. They didn't need words.

Tasha knew.

. . .

"IT WAS A BEAUTIFUL CEREMONY," DYLAN SAID FROM behind him. Pushing back the instant thrill that Dylan was here, Lucas schooled his features into a smile and turned to face the man who had filled his thoughts for the past hour or so.

"It was," Lucas murmured. Dylan took a step closer until there were only inches between them. He remained dressed as he had been for the entire ceremony as official photographer. "Are you not bartending tonight?"

Dylan pointed at his own chest and shook his head. "Official photographer today, gets me out of working at the bar. Scott is covering for me. Where did your sister and her husband go? Have they moved into the honeymoon cabin?"

"About half an hour ago."

"Do you need to stay here?"

"Here?" Lucas wasn't following the conversation.

"Here with the wedding party." Dylan gestured around him as he asked. Lucas followed the movement. Most of the party had split into couples and wandered off in their own directions.

"My job here is done," Lucas deadpanned. The humor in his voice made Dylan smile.

"Then can I show you something?"

"Is this where you offer to show me your etchings so you can have your wicked way with me?" Lucas was safe using humor—it was a good shield and one that worked in all situations.

"No," Dylan began in all seriousness. Lucas stiffened. Had he offended him? Typical. One hot guy, a warm night, starlight, endless possibilities, and he fucks it up with his freaky dry, sarcastic sense of what was funny.

"No?" He tried to hold back the disappointment. He wasn't sure how far he wanted this meet up to go but he had hoped for some more of that hot sexy kissing at least.

"No." Dylan leaned in so that his mouth was no more than an inch from Lucas's ear. "This is where I take you for a walk to show you one of my favorite places on earth and then we make out under the stars under the privacy of the dark." Dylan's voice was husky and there was no joking in his words. He was deadly serious. Holding out his hand very deliberately, he continued, "So, can I show you something?"

Mesmerized by the sex dripping from Dylan's voice and the utter need that flooded him at that point, Lucas was incapable of saying no. Reaching out and gripping Dylan's hand, he simply nodded.

Dylan pulled one of the lanterns from the tree. Inside was a pillar candle, and he passed it to Lucas before helping himself to another. Quietly, he led Lucas to the shoreline and then turned left—away from the main complex, the pool, the people, and most importantly, in the opposite direction to the honeymoon cabin he knew his sister was in.

"It's not far," Dylan explained. "There is this place here, a crop of stone and a plateau and it's fed by a natural warm spring." The whole thing was a surreal experience. From the gentle whooshing of waves to the sweep of the light from the candles, everything served to help Lucas relax.

"We're here," he said. He needn't have said a word.

Lucas froze on the spot and stared, open-mouthed. Lit only by moonlight and the gentle candle glimmer, the formed rocks were simply dark shapes against the night. He blinked as he searched for the water, but it was only when Dylan pulled him a few more steps that he saw what it was Dylan wanted him to see. The sound of running water was hypnotic and there were no words between them as Dylan helped Lucas to the rocks above the water. They sat on the rock with legs dangling for a moment.

"It's warm," Lucas said wonderingly.

"It's heated by the sun all day, but we think there is natural warm spring water here. I found it the first day I came to the island. Found this and a shack I sometimes sleep in when I'm here and I need space." Dylan pointed somewhere to the left, but Lucas couldn't see anything. Maybe he was indicating back to the group of staff cabins that housed the twenty of so people it took to run the island.

"How long have you been visiting here? Working here?"

"This summer is my fifth summer."

"Did you come here first as a vacation? With family?"

Dylan shook his head. "Not a vacation. I was traveling and I found the water taxi and I asked the guy running it if the place he was going had work. There's the man who runs this place, Antoine—"

"I spoke to him when I was organizing payment."

"Yeah. Him. Well, he and his wife own and run the island. He was ferrying a wedding party to Sapphire Cay, and he said they did have seasonal work if I wanted it. I went with him and I stayed a long time—at least until the sun went." Dylan nodded and then turned his attention back to the water. Conversation was clearly closed down at that point about all things Dylan. Lucas pondered the cryptic statement but didn't say anything. Dylan didn't need to share everything if he didn't want to. Dylan shrugged off his shirt and pants until he was just in his shorts, and after a small hesitation Lucas did the same thing. After all, his cotton shorts gave no less modesty than swim trunks.

"I'm going in," Dylan said. "Follow my path if you want, it can be slippery and dangerous sometimes."

Carefully, Lucas picked the same steps as Dylan and sighed as the warm water enveloped him. The base of the pool was made up of smooth stones and sand under his feet and he slid into the water until he was fully submerged. Staying that way until his lungs told him that they had had enough, he finally pushed his feet against the bottom and floated to the surface. The depth was just slightly shallower than his five ten and when he shook the water from his eyes, he could see Dylan breaking the water after doing the same as him.

Experimentally, Lucas tasted the water on his lips—salty, but not as much as the sea, which supported the hypothesis that this was a naturally fed spring. Interesting on an island in the middle of the sea. Lucas resolved to check that on the internet when he got back to the mainland. Together they lay back and floated. The stars were so damn bright and clear, and ignoring the insistent nagging ache in his stomach, he let the peace of this place wash over him.

As they floated they bumped hands, and Dylan told

stories about other weddings, where a guest ending up in the pool—like Kate had—was the least of the problems.

"Then, she took off her dress, right there on the beach. There was no underwear, literally none, and her new husband was saying 'keep taking the damn photos'. I didn't know where to look. Apparently, she wanted to be at one with nature or something, and then when he stripped as well and they posed I just went with the flow."

"What about the rest of the guests?"

"Let's just say the bride was beautiful and her husband was easy on the eyes, but most of the party should have kept their clothes on."

Lucas laughed at the feigned horror in Dylan's voice. "So you just kept shooting photos?"

"For half an hour. Then to add insult to injury, it's me that edits the photos, so I had to look at it all over again. That's when I noticed that in the background of some of the shots the bride and groom had used the shelter of the biggest tree to express their joy in very different ways. With the best man included."

"You're joking."

"I can show you the photos."

"No!" Lucas exclaimed and then laughed. "Thanks, but no."

"The best man was kind of hot though. Way past gorgeous. All muscles and dark brooding eyes. Sex on legs, if you know what I mean." Dylan's voice was low and dripped with lascivious huskiness and Lucas imagined him waggling his eyebrows.

Just from the words alone, Lucas could imagine that

other man in this water with Dylan. Damn his overactive imagination.

"He was?" Sudden doubt filled Lucas's thoughts. He needed to tamp down the attraction. This had to be nothing more than mutual sex and relieving the tension that swirled in his head. He was nothing special. Who was he kidding thinking Dylan hadn't done this before? He'd been here for five summers, probably had every single type of wedding party on the beach. Of course he'd been attracted to other guests. Lucas was unlikely to be the first or the last. Letting his legs sink, Lucas stood and stretched tall.

"I need to be getting back," he said while trying not to sound like a hurt kid who was trying to be brave. Dylan copied his movement and stopped Lucas with a touch of his hand.

"What's wrong?"

"Nothing."

"We were talking. What did I say?"

"Nothing."

"You're saying the word 'nothing' a lot here."

"What else do you want me to say?" Irritation built inside Lucas. He hated it when he lost the ability to actually form real sentences. It only happened when he was around men he desired past just the talking stage. He got all tongue-tied and overcautious.

"You could start by telling me what is making you so sad in this beautiful place where your sister just got married, and you have nothing to think about except blue skies and calm seas. Or you could tell me why you're leaving now?"

"You said… you told me… fuck."

"What? That I would show you the photos?"

Dylan sounded genuinely confused and Lucas bit his tongue to keep from just spilling out his disappointment. He needed to think this one through.

"It's been good here. I needed this," he said finally. He changed the conversation even though he knew it was a cop out. He needed peace in his life more than his next breath and he was thankful he had enjoyed some calm moments when even the ache in his stomach had seemed to ease. "Thank you," he tagged on the end. Then he took a few steps away from Dylan and made to leave.

"Was it because I said the best man was hot?"

Lucas stopped in his tracks. He had almost two weeks to live on this island, possibly seeing Dylan every single damn day. If he was honest now then he had nowhere to run to. He could quite easily stand here up to his neck in warm water and spill everything in a torrent of indecision and stress.

"Yes," he finally said. That was enough. Dylan didn't need to know why it had unnerved him.

"Hmmm" was all Dylan said. In an instant, he took the two steps to stand right next to Lucas, and in surprise Lucas stumbled and slipped on the stone. Dylan grabbed him quickly and steadied him. "Okay?" he asked gently.

Lucas shrugged free. "Thank you." He should leave now, but something stopped him from moving. It could be anything from the romantic wash of moonlight on Dylan's face to the fear of losing his balance again, but whatever it was had him frozen in place. The water eddied and rippled around him and his skin felt touched in a million places by the luxury of warm silk.

Dylan reached out of the water and cupped Lucas's face between his palms. His skin was cool and the droplets from his touch tracked down over his chin and into the water. The move was sudden but Lucas didn't flinch.

"Five years I have come here and I have never wanted to kiss another guest."

"Uh huh?"

"Never seen so much sadness in another man, or pain in his eyes."

"Oh." That was literally all Lucas could manage.

"Can I kiss you, Lucas Madison?" He leaned closer and Lucas instinctively mirrored the action. For a second their gazes locked and Lucas wished it were lighter so he could see Dylan's eyes more clearly.

"Please…"

Dylan pressed cool, damp lips against his and the touch was perfect. It had been so long since Lucas had kissed another man and now he had kissed Dylan twice. So caught up in work, there had been nothing and no one he wanted to share this most intimate of touches with. For a short time, they simply pressed their lips together, and then with a sigh Lucas tilted his head and opened his mouth for more. Dylan pressed his hands against Lucas and deepened the kiss. The tangle of tongues, the taste of the other man was intoxicating, and all Lucas could do was hang on for the ride. He couldn't remember ever being with someone and spending so much time on kissing alone. Spreading his legs for a more solid balance, he moved his hands through the water and rested them on Dylan's hipbones.

He could stand here forever.

Chapter Six

GOD, HE COULD HAPPILY DO THIS ALL NIGHT, DYLAN thought as he gently caressed Lucas's face as they kissed. In fact, if they managed all night, it would just leave him wanting more. The erotic touch stole away his breath and, accompanied by Lucas's fingers caressing the skin across his shoulders and back, Dylan swore he was going to lose his mind.

"I want to show you something," Dylan said between kisses, and he dropped his hands beneath the surface of the water to gently take hold of Lucas's hips. He moved his fingers upward and brushed pale, sensitive skin. A smile curled his lips as Lucas flinched beneath his touch.

"More? What?" Lucas asked. He looked at Dylan, though by the dreamy expression on his face, he'd go along with any reasonable suggestion.

Dylan smiled and pulled Lucas close. "Something good. I promise." He caught Lucas's lower lip with his teeth and gave it a soft nip. Drawing Lucas into a firm kiss,

Dylan held him tightly and slowly began to guide him forward through the water. Their lips remained locked as Dylan turned them around until Lucas was backed up against the rocks on the far side of the pool. Breathing in deeply, Dylan reluctantly pulled back. He met Lucas's eyes through his lashes and smiled. There was something different than before about the man looking back at him. The sadness had been lifted, if only slightly. He could almost be fooled into thinking everything was suddenly okay. But looks were often deceiving.

"It's getting late," Lucas whispered, suddenly putting on the brakes. He looked at Dylan and wore a thoughtful expression. What was Lucas thinking? The lusty glaze had cleared from his eyes and he leaned back against the rocks. Maybe Dylan shouldn't have mentioned the best man. Was it still bothering Lucas?

Dylan reached past Lucas and pressed them to the smooth rock behind him. Lucas must have had fun, right? They'd kissed and touched and even talked. It had all been pretty easy. The two of them had fallen into a rhythm, their bodies pressing and grinding against each other as they sought comfort and friction. If Lucas wanted more, Dylan would happily oblige. It would just be sex after all. There was no need to overthink this. Didn't matter if Lucas was really the first man Dylan had been attracted to in a long time. Lucas just needed to relax. Two men, one night, that's all it had to be. If that was what Lucas needed then Dylan was okay with that.

"You have somewhere to be tomorrow?" he asked and pressed his mouth briefly to Lucas's. Lucas looked unsure.

So, no sex tonight. No matter. Dylan still wanted to be there. That was more than enough. "Ten minutes. Scout's honor?" He gave an encouraging smile.

"You were a boy scout?" Lucas asked and leaned back. There was a spark of intrigue behind his eyes. "So, you're pretty handy at putting up a tent or lighting a campfire?"

Dylan shook his head. He never did any of that as a kid. Between hospital appointments and recovery, he'd missed most of his childhood. He'd missed out on a lot of things, and that was something he had strived to correct.

"I was too busy doing nothing," he stated and cleared his throat. Getting hung up on all that crap was never his thing. Him, Mom, and Dad, it was a sad little tale he didn't intend on sharing right now. "Come on. It won't take long."

Hesitating at first, Lucas finally agreed. "Okay. For a little while." He rubbed at his eyes and sighed as he turned to get out of the water.

Pressing his mouth in a line, Dylan watched as Lucas climbed the rocks. Water hung heavily in the material of Lucas's shorts, which in turn clung and formed around his ass. He enjoyed the view for a moment, until he realized Lucas was looking back over his shoulder.

"You are coming, right?" he asked.

"Er, yeah." Quickly, Dylan followed the path Lucas had taken out of the water and got to his feet. He glanced back at the calm pool as he pulled at the waistband of his shorts. The thin material was unlikely to take long to dry but it wasn't the most comfortable of sensations against skin. The night air was cool but edged with the muggy heat from the afternoon. He offered his hand to Lucas and felt a warmth spread through his chest as Lucas took it. "This way," he said and guided Lucas between the trees.

It didn't take long to find what he wanted to show Lucas, and he breathed in deeply as the trees thinned out and the space opened up a little. He looked fondly at the building in the clearing. It was his, and until now, he had never brought anyone else out there. Not in the way he'd brought Lucas. Sure, Antoine and Jeanie and a few of the staff knew about it, but they pretty much stayed away. This was his space. Somewhere to clear his head and spend quality time with no one else but himself.

"What is this place?" Lucas asked as he slipped his hand from Dylan's loose hold and walked up to the shack. He stood for a moment and wrapped his hand around the wooden beam supporting the left-hand side of the roof.

The building was split into two parts, an open veranda area and then a small room on the right. Its walls and roof were a mixture of wood and corrugated steel sheets that Dylan had slowly rebuilt over the last few years.

"It's mine," Dylan said with pride and walked past Lucas. He flashed him a smile as he pushed open the light wooden door, which creaked on its hinges as it swung inside the small room. "I usually come here when I want to be alone. Everyone here's great, but sometimes I just need that extra space, ya know?"

Lucas nodded and slowly followed Dylan inside. "I guess I do."

Dylan crossed the shack to the small desk pushed up against the far wall. On top of the desk were an oil-burning lamp and a Ziploc bag. "It's so quiet and peaceful," he continued as he picked up the plastic bag and turned to lean against the hard edge. He slowly began to empty the bag, reaching behind him as he placed each item on the desk—a notebook and pen, a dog-eared paperback of the Iliad, and a box of matches. "And if you listen really hard, you can hear the water filling the pool. It's kind of therapeutic. It's like the rest of the world disappears." He lowered his head as he realized Lucas was watching him. Sliding open the matchbox, he took a match and then lit the lamp. An orange glow flooded the room and Dylan noted how it flattered Lucas. Years seemed to be chased away from Lucas's face and it added some much-needed color to his cheeks.

"Do you come here often?" Lucas asked and then smiled as Dylan crossed to the small cot that stood behind the door and indicated for Lucas to join him. There was a rough towel and he passed it over to wipe away the worst of the water.

"Is that some kind of pick-up line?" Dylan teased and hung the lamp on a hook above the bed.

"Oh, no. I didn't mean…"

Dylan laughed as embarrassment colored Lucas's face.

"Sorry," Lucas said with a sigh and sat down beside Dylan. "But do you?"

What did Lucas consider often? Since returning to the island, Dylan had maybe come out here four or five times, and all of those visits had been in the last couple of weeks. Things with Dad were making him dizzy. He wasn't interested in signing papers and money. He just wasn't that guy.

"Just now and then." Dylan chewed on the inside of his

mouth. "It's a tropical island with white beaches, blue sky, and warm seas. What could possibly bother me out here?" *What indeed?* He focused on Lucas. They were dealing with Lucas's issues—not his.

Lucas shrugged. "Life has a nasty habit of catching up."

Shaking his head, Dylan laughed. "Maybe if you stop carrying your damn cell around, it wouldn't." He grinned as he turned to face Lucas. "It'd probably have to be surgically detached though, right?"

Lucas's eyes brightened as his gaze met Dylan's, and Dylan thought it was one of the most beautiful things he'd ever seen. The hazel sparked with a golden glow from the lamp's flame and Dylan could no longer resist the urge to lean in and kiss Lucas again. Tenderly, Dylan kissed and touched and teased Lucas into a warm embrace. Holding the tops of Lucas's arms, he guided Lucas back across the bed and pulled him close. Lucas burrowed into the hold, and wrapped close, they simply held each other. They lay together silently for a while, kissing and sharing soothing touches to heated skin until exhausted, they eventually fell asleep.

DYLAN GROANED AS HE AWKWARDLY STRETCHED OUT HIS arms and squirmed against the mattress. Blinking, he breathed in deeply, lifted his head from the flat pillow, and opened his eyes. The otherwise pitch-black shack was illuminated by the low light of the oil lamp, and Dylan wondered how long they had been there. Lucas's warmth had relaxed him and lulled him into a peaceful slumber. He didn't have any idea of the time, but he knew he couldn't stay here all night. Smiling, he leaned over and looked at Lucas, who looked a hell of a lot better and more chilled out than he had been. Sleep—another good medicine.

Reluctantly, Dylan slid from between the wall and Lucas and got off the end of the cot. He didn't want to disturb Lucas, but he wasn't sure how the other man might take waking up to a note on the pillow. Quietly, he crouched down beside Lucas's head and gently began stroking back Lucas's bangs. Drawing soothing lines back and forth across Lucas's forehead, Dylan eventually coaxed Lucas awake.

"Hey," he whispered as Lucas looked at him, slightly disoriented. "Sorry to wake you, but I need to get back."

"What time is it?" Lucas asked as he yawned.

"No idea." Dylan smiled and gently ran his hand over Lucas's shoulder. "Do you want me to walk you back, or can you find your own way?"

Lucas closed his eyes and hugged the pillow. "I'll find my own way," he murmured.

Getting to his feet, Dylan leaned down and pressed his lips to Lucas's cheek. "I'll go find your clothes and bring them in. You sure you'll be okay?"

"It's an island," Lucas mumbled as he rolled onto his stomach. "How lost could I get?"

Dylan snorted a laugh. "Just head back the way we came and down to the beach," he offered. "Follow the shore and you'll see the walkway and the lights of the hotel."

"I'll be fine," Lucas said and opened his eyes briefly as he smiled. "Thanks."

Dylan nodded. "Later," he said and backed toward the door. He didn't want to leave, but there was something he needed to do.

THE NIGHT AIR WAS COOL AND REFRESHING AS DYLAN made his way along the water's edge. He watched the white foam circle his feet for a second time as the tide continued its advance up the sand. He guessed it must be around ten. The sound of music from the wedding reception could still be heard, and he figured it couldn't have been more than a couple of hours since he stole Lucas away from the drinks and celebrations. Swerving, he took a shortcut through some trees and made his way around the back of the hotel to the staff cabins. Away from the music, Dylan appreciated the silence as he slipped inside his cabin. He closed his eyes as he stood in the middle of his room and took a deep breath. Crossing to his dresser, he picked up the old Nokia and checked the screen. Three messages since that morning. He opened the first and read the message from his father's secretary. *Shit.* Dad had gotten impatient.

Representative M Stone at airport for signing, 11 p.m.

Damn. The message had been sent at ten that morning, and what the hell? Stone? Mitch Stone? Great, just what Dylan needed right now, an ex-lover showing up. He was sure his dad would have done it on purpose, maybe even considered Mitch a way of luring Dylan back home.

He continued onto the next message.

I assume your dad was in touch. I don't want things to be awkward between us. The flight's due at 10:40. It'll be good to see you.

Fuck it all. Dylan hadn't seen or spoken to Mitch in almost six years. He'd been nineteen and in lust. Mitch worked as an intern for Dylan's father and they'd kind of had a thing for a couple of months. Their relationship was before Dylan decided he couldn't pretend any more about being the man his father wanted. Suits and cell phones, money and deals were not for him. He didn't want a nine-to-five like his dad; though in reality it was more of a seven-to-ten job. They had rarely seen each other in the years before Dylan moved out.

With a heavy sigh, Dylan read the final message.

Flight on time. See you around 11.

Dylan's gaze drifted to the time on the screen. It was already after half past ten. "Crap," he grumbled and pinched the bridge of his nose as he tried to figure out where the wonderfully relaxed person he'd been only moments ago had vanished to. His dad had been reminding him of the documents on and off for the last couple of months, but Dylan had consigned them to the back of his mind with the many other 'do for Dad' things that had cropped up in the last five years. How important could this stuff possibly be? Paperwork, signatures, and money—he was doing perfectly fine without any of them. His dad, however, seemed desperate for him to sign and had now sent Mitch on some late night venture. Dylan guessed he only had himself to blame, after all, he had done everything he could to put the man off, even said he couldn't agree to a daylight hours meeting. Anything to avoid the inevitable.

Running late. Be there in an hour, he sent back.

That would have to be enough. Quickly, he got a change of clothes and ran a comb through his tangled hair. Shaking his head, he tried to brush out the faint spatter of sand that had dried in his bangs before brushing them back and behind his ears. He wasn't sure why he cared about his appearance, it should take an hour tops to read and sign what his dad needed. Grabbing the keys to the boat, he headed out and down to the dock. The quicker he did this, the sooner he could get back to enjoying his life.

"I'M SO SORRY I'M LATE," DYLAN SAID, TRYING TO SOUND genuine. He wasn't sorry. If he thought he'd get away with it, he wouldn't have shown up at all. But the last thing Dylan wanted was for anyone linked to his dad turning up on the island that he could have avoided with a trip to the mainland.

Mitch Stone looked exactly as Dylan remembered him —slicked-back blond hair, piercing blue eyes, a slim-fit gray suit covering his gym-toned body, and model-perfect cheekbones and jaw. Dylan quashed the twinge of attraction that lurched in his chest—it wasn't anything other than muscle memory. Mitch was as cold as his blue gaze and Dylan didn't need someone like that in his life, he reminded himself. He'd played second-best too many times already—to his father and to Mitch—and he wasn't willing to do it again.

"Only an hour," Mitch huffed as he got to his feet and picked his briefcase up off the floor.

"At least I texted." Dylan met Mitch's eyes and knew the man was well aware of what he was getting at. Mitch had been just like Dylan's father. Work was an excuse to be late or to not show at all.

Mitch pressed his lips in a firm line before checking his watch. Yes, Dylan was beyond late, but this hadn't been his idea. Mitch could thank Dylan's father.

Dylan really hoped this was going to be quick. "So, where are we doing this?" he asked and eyed the briefcase that no doubt contained several papers for him to read and sign.

"I fly back out in the morning," Mitch said. "I have a room booked at a hotel. We can go there."

I don't think so. "What needs doing?" Dylan hadn't quite got his head around what it was he was actually signing. At his birth, Dylan's father had invested money for his son and it was due to mature ten days after Dylan's twenty-fifth birthday. His birthday was tomorrow. Mitch sat back down and rested the briefcase on his knees. "The policy your father took out for you is due to mature. For payment to be made to you, your signature is needed alongside your father's. This will then go into your trust, which is due to be transferred to you next week." He opened the briefcase and took out a pile of papers. "At eighteen you deferred the claim on your trust until you reached twenty-five. With this investment, you're looking at just shy of a million."

What? "You're serious?"

Holding out the papers, Mitch gave a short nod. "Yes."

Dylan gave a breathy laugh. A fucking million? What the hell? He sat down next to Mitch and took the papers. Scanning the details, he found Mitch was telling the truth. "I can't believe it." In the last six years, he'd insisted on doing everything himself. He moved from place to place taking any crappy job that would pay his way, and then he would move on to the next. He hadn't given a crap what was in the account when he was eighteen. He didn't want it then.

"Can I defer again?"

"You could," Mitch shrugged. "But do you want to spend the rest of your life thinking on this? Maybe you should just sign, take the money, and give it to charity."

Shit. Maybe that is what should happen. Money doesn't replace love and affection. "How long do I have to think about it?"

"My flight's at nine forty-five in the morning. It needs to be signed by then." Mitch looked at him and narrowed his eyes. "I'm not really getting what the issue is, D."

Dylan stared at the first name on the document. Maria Gray. He had never gotten the chance to meet his mother. Sure, he'd seen hundreds of photos and even dared to see her in his own reflection. They shared the same eye and hair coloring and the same straight nose. He often wondered if that was why his father had done everything he could to avoid him as he was growing up. Who would want to see their dead wife's face in that of the person who had killed her? Dylan cleared his throat. He knew that wasn't true. Life was just cruel sometimes. And then his dad had had to go through it all over again with the cancer that had nearly killed Dylan in childhood.

"Dylan?"

"Sorry," Dylan said and handed the papers back to Mitch as he got to his feet. "I can't do this right now."

"What? Why?" Mitch looked up at Dylan, obviously confused.

How could he ever understand? "I just… It's a lot of money."

Mitch's expression seemed to soften. "She'd want you to have it."

Dylan met Mitch's eyes. He couldn't remember if they'd ever talked about his mother. His chest ached at the memory of stories his father had told him. There had been some complication during the birth—his birth—and she'd died. "You think? I imagine she'd rather be here and alive." He licked at his dry lower lip and turned around to stare out the large glass front of the airport. He took a deep breath and tried to calm himself down. Through the years of doctors and appointments and drugs and treatments, all he ever wanted was his mom. Everyone told him how she was an angel up in heaven looking down on him and keeping him safe through the cancer.

"Of course she would. But sadly, she isn't. So she'd want you to be happy."

Snorting a laugh, Dylan turned back around. Mitch was just like Dylan's dad. Both thought money was the answer to everything, including a soul's happiness. He looked at Mitch and then at the papers. He didn't have to touch the money, he figured, or maybe he could do something good with it. That would have made his mom happy. Charity? Or an investment in something. Anything. He didn't need it.

"Do you have a pen?" he finally said.

Mitch quickly opened and closed his briefcase and held out a black ballpoint to Dylan. He gave a small smile as Dylan took it and came back to sit beside him.

"Okay," Dylan said. "Where do I sign?"

Chapter Seven

LUCAS WOKE TO LIGHT FLOODING THE CABIN THROUGH THE various nooks and crannies in the aged wood. The waking hadn't been sudden, more a delicious stretch and curl into the mattress and the thought of having nowhere to be. Dylan had left; he knew that. Blinking, he realized he couldn't recall when other than it had been dark. Stretching again, he looked up at the roof and marveled that the thing had survived any of the storms that made their way across this stretch of ocean in hurricane season. The whole structure was a patchwork of wood and iron and both old and new nails. The main struts looked to be tied together with rope, which probably made the whole thing less rigid and more able to withstand the bending breaking forces of nature.

Moving outside, he realized the shack was protected on all sides by natural bluffs of rock, and just a few short steps later, he was back by the body of water Dylan had taken him to last night. The water was mirror-smooth at the edges, and he could see clearly the small wannabe waterfall that fed the natural bowl in the sand. Memories flooded him of the taste of Dylan, of his touch and the confident way that he led him to the water and then back to the shack. Butterflies made themselves known in his stomach and his chest tightened when he recalled each touch.

Following the shoreline, he made it back to the hotel in good time and slipped into his cabin before anyone could see him, if indeed anyone was up. The complex was quiet, although the smell of bacon wafted through the open area and by the silent swimming pool. First order was to get a shower. His skin was crusty with sand and his hair felt coarse with both sand and dried seawater.

The shower was hot, and inch by inch he relaxed into the flow and then rested his head on folded arms against the wall, allowing the water to beat down on his back. The burn of acid in his gut was back, and reluctantly he left the shower, wrapping a towel around his waist and locating his meds in his bag. Two tablets for this, a pill for that, several others as vitamins. Jesus, he was a walking fricking pharmacy. It was time to stop drinking and get on them. He had made it through the wedding, done his bit, drunk the toasts, even loosened up a bit, but now he had to settle the pain.

After dressing casually in Bermuda shorts and a loose purple T-shirt, he paced his room restlessly. Every now and again, he stopped at the room safe. Inside were his netbook and the papers he needed to review. He could even imagine himself opening the safe and pulling out what he needed to work. Tasha would shout at him, but hell, he needed to get the initial review sent back to Municipal before he left Sapphire Cay. He just didn't want to. He wanted to find Dylan and thank him for the best night's sleep he had experienced since he was studying for his degree. Decision made, he pocketed his cell—his only concession to having his finger on the pulse—and made his way to the breakfast room. His cell showed it to be only six a.m. and he doubted anyone from last night was going to be up. Bride and groom safely ensconced in their honeymoon cabin meant the rest of the party could enjoy the alcohol on tap. He probably missed out on a hell of a lot more dumpings into the pool.

"Morning, Mr. Madison," a voice greeted him. Lucas turned to see Antoine Durand sitting at a side table with papers piled next to him and his wife, Jeanie, sitting opposite him with a ready smile on her beautiful face.

"Morning," Lucas said. He returned the smile. These two were nice people. The contact he had exchanged with them had mostly been by email, but even in those written words he had felt the warmth and welcome.

"Did you sleep well?" Jeanie asked. Lucas nodded and glanced quickly at her expression. He suddenly felt she knew he hadn't been in his room, and for some unaccountable reason he felt guilty. Did everyone know? Were people laughing at him? Had he fucked up?

Shit.

Forcing calming breaths and focusing on her expression, he saw nothing but a friendly question and no hidden meaning in the softly accented words. Fucking panic attacks and the constant feeling of fucking up... now he even suspected gently spoken questions.

"Please join us," Antoine offered. "We are the only ones here and the coffee is hot."

Lucas immediately opened his mouth to decline. He didn't want the company; he didn't do socializing and he didn't want anyone to feel that they had to sit with him. Before he could say anything, Antoine had scooted around to sit next to his wife, who smiled at him and moved a little to give him room. Seemed Lucas had no choice.

When Jeanie poured fresh coffee into a clean mug the deal was struck. Lucas would push past his fears about knowing what the hell to talk about and sit and eat his damn breakfast with two people who didn't have an agenda or want anything from him.

Sliding into the recently vacated space, he brought the coffee to his lips and inhaled the scent of it before sipping at the steaming brew. Nectar touched his tongue and slid sinuously down his throat. Coffee on an empty stomach wasn't entirely a good thing, but hell, this was perfect caffeine. Fluffy eggs and biscuits were scooped onto a plate and passed to him, and before he knew it he was talking between mouthfuls about the wedding and his sister and the island. He couldn't help but see the papers on the corner of the desk and his innate curiosity won out.

"You're selling Sapphire Cay?" he finally asked. The top sheet listing the island with an associated view from the air wasn't exactly subtle. Nor was the seven-hundred-thousand-dollar price tag. It didn't seem a lot for such a slice of beauty.

"When we first purchased the Cay it cost us very little and had nothing much more than a shack at one end," began Jeanie. Lucas idly wondered if that was Dylan's shack she spoke of. "My father invested a little and we opened a year later."

"I was so young," Antoine said. He shook his head. "And look at us now." He laughed and Jeanie leaned into him. The show of support and affection sent a stab of jealousy through Lucas. He missed seeing his mom and dad being so naturally affectionate and it wasn't likely he would ever be in a relationship where he could experience that same level of ease.

"Getting too old," Jeanie said softly.

"You're not old," Lucas protested. Politeness dictated he say that, but he wasn't lying. Her blonde hair was short and soft and her skin was not lined in the way a normal sixty-year-old might be.

"We have to take the best chance at retiring now and we think it's time to move on. Give someone else the chance to enjoy Sapphire Cay."

"Seven hundred doesn't seem like a lot of money for all of this." Lucas waved a hand to indicate the cabins and the main rooms and the beaches and pools. The whole island was stunning. Antoine tapped the pile of papers.

"Expenses mount quickly. We break even every year but we have nothing in reserve. You know how it goes. Not only that, but there are repairs that need doing. Our son Jamie used to take care of that but he hasn't been here for four years now, and getting someone in who knows what they're doing is expensive. So we are not selling a money spinner that will make someone rich." He shrugged like it wasn't an important observation, but Lucas knew how difficult times had been to make money, let alone in the tourism industry.

"Do you have any buyers?"

Antoine looked at his wife briefly, for what reason Lucas couldn't ascertain. Support? Understanding? Love?

"We had one person we were hoping would..." He trailed off and shook his head. "Never mind. He said no and I don't blame him. To live here on this island, to make it a place people like your sister want to get married, a stunning backdrop and making beautiful memories, it takes a special person, special people."

Lucas concentrated on his breakfast for a while. He wondered if he could manage to stay on an island, come thick or thin, for what must be well over thirty years like Antoine and Jeanie. There was internet here, albeit sketchy internet. Cell phones worked here. There was an office here. But... No. If he got out, then he had to find a way to make money, away from nebulous thoughts of paradise, otherwise he would have nothing for his future. As it stood, to leave Municipal with no immediate job to go to would dent his savings and investments. Idly, he rubbed his chest.

"You had children on the island though?" he finally said and then felt uncomfortable when he realized that he had spoken that aloud and interrupted whatever they had been saying.

"Two." Jeanie smiled. She clearly hadn't been worried about his blurted question. "A boy and a girl. Both were at school on the mainland."

"Neither of them want to take over?"

"Sue is a doctor in Miami, happily married with two children. Jamie is in the military."

"He's away in Afghanistan," Antoine offered. There was pride in his voice. "He's a Marine."

Lucas wondered how to respond to that one. "You must be very proud of them both," he finally offered.

"We are. Scared some about Jamie, though," Jeanie added. She looked down at her coffee but not before Lucas caught a flash of fear in her eyes.

"He's gay you see," Antoine said. "Doesn't matter about DADT being repealed, it isn't easy for him to be in Afghanistan, but the Marine Corps is like a family." Lucas watched the expressions on Antoine's face. He wasn't entirely sure Antoine believed what he was saying—that the Corps was a family to replace the one that Jamie wouldn't have because he was away from home. But whatever, it seemed to help Antoine some.

"It isn't easy for anyone over there," Lucas said. He wasn't going to be drawn into a heavy conversation on Don't-Ask-Don't-Tell or anything he really knew nothing about.

"Would you like to see some photos?" Jeanie asked. She pushed herself up and away from the table, which interrupted Lucas's automatic need to refuse. Pictures of other people's kids, however cute, weren't something he was an expert in looking at. He couldn't wait to be an uncle, but that was different.

Which is why he was left wondering what the hell happened when he left the table two hours later with a grin on his face. Not only that, but he was feeling nearly as relaxed as he had been in Dylan's arms last night. The stories that the couple told and the photos he looked at were fun and interesting, and he resolved to dig out his own family albums as soon as he was home. He thought Tasha had them. He had to ask.

"Morning, gorgeous."

Dylan's voice, like smooth whisky, came from somewhere behind him and Lucas spun on his heel to face the very man who filled his thoughts.

"Hey," he offered almost shyly.

"Do you want to get breakfast?"

Regret filled him and he glanced down at the time. Even he couldn't manage two breakfasts. Still, the offer of sitting opposite Dylan was enough for him to say he could kill for coffee. He wasn't lying. He could, in fact, kill anyone that got in between him and his coffee. Dylan didn't have to know he had already had three cups, along with two plates of food.

"I've already eaten," he admitted, "but I'd love more coffee."

He just hoped Antoine and Jeanie didn't spot him stealing back into the restaurant for more; manners made him not want to appear too greedy. As it turned out, they wouldn't since Dylan took him out the back to the kitchen and set out two coffees on a long stainless steel counter. The kitchen was L-shaped and even though Lucas could hear movement and work from the main part, in this area there was quiet. Dylan trapped him between the counter and his body and drew him into a breath-stealing kiss. Lucas lifted his hands and twisted his fingers into Dylan's soft, curly hair. The kiss deepened and Dylan half lifted, half helped Lucas onto the edge of the counter. He swiftly moved into the V of Lucas's spread legs and only then did Lucas feel just how much Dylan wanted to be close. They were both hard and their dicks rubbed against each other, their tongues tangling and teasing until there was more laughter than heat. One small move, though, and heat flared through Lucas again. *Fuck.* If they weren't careful he was going to come in his briefs just from the kissing and the teasing.

Finally, Dylan appeared to want to slow everything down and he eased away, although they were still pressed hard against each other at groin level.

"Good morning," he said.

"Morning," Lucas replied. He wanted more of the frankly awesome kissing and maybe a little more rubbing.

"I wish we weren't in a kitchen with the chef around the corner," Dylan commented dryly. Lucas blinked at the words. Kitchen? People? He had kind of blanked out both. Finally, he closed his eyes and rested his forehead against Dylan's.

"Me too," he admitted.

"I'm not on until five today. It's a couple of hours to high tide. Do you want to go snorkeling?"

The invitation was impromptu. Lucas thought very quickly. Dylan wore such a hopeful expression that Lucas could feel his resolve melt away entirely. He had work to do, but the idea of more half-naked Dylan was worth putting that to one side.

"I've never done it before," he admitted. He attempted to keep the nerves out of his voice. He loved swimming, he loved water, but he hated not knowing what to do.

Being capable was ingrained into him. Even admitting he didn't know how to snorkel smarted a bit.

"Even better then, I get to show you. Meet you by the pool in ten?" With a last kiss Dylan left him sitting on the counter and, whistling, pushed his way through the swinging doors and disappeared. For a second, Lucas simply sat and watched the space where the force of nature that was Dylan had been standing. His lips tingled from the kiss, the taste of the other man was in his mouth, and the evidence of his arousal tented his loose shorts if anyone cared to look. Adjusting himself discretely, he too left the kitchen, and if he heard the chef chuckling behind him then he chose to ignore it.

DYLAN LAY BACK ON THE SAND IN THE SHADE OF A large palm away from the hotel and off the beaten track and Lucas followed suit. They were using the excuse of the sudden downfall of warm rain as a reason to hide away from prying eyes. The last few hours of snorkeling had been restful and exhilarating at the same time, and had been a fantastic way to celebrate Dylan turning twenty-five. They had seen evidence of an old wooden dock that had subsided and been claimed by the sea and schools of yellowtail snappers that swam in and out of the old wood. Upside-down jellyfish and boxfish moved lazily in the shallows, and inside the parts that had once supported the dock were spider crabs and red-banded shrimp. Scorpion fish, camouflaged on the bottom, darted here and there when disturbed, and all the while

Dylan had been there with a hand on him to guide and teach.

"We should go out at night," Dylan said. His voice was sleepy-slow and his features relaxed. "We could set up an underwater light and watch. At night, everything is on the move in the sea; crawfish, octopi, sleeping parrot fish, snake eels—you name it, we have it." Dylan yawned widely and closed his eyes. On impulse, Lucas straddled Dylan and placed a hand either side of his head on the sand.

"Thank you," he said.

Dylan didn't move nor did he encourage Lucas to move off him. Ass to groin, they sat looking at each other for a second. Dylan all of a sudden looked very awake and he blinked up at Lucas.

"Lucas?" he said gently. There were a wealth of questions in that simple word.

"Let's go back to my cabin." That was possibly the bravest thing Lucas had ever said to another person in his life. He didn't know what Dylan would say.

"Why?" Dylan replied gently.

"I want to…" His words failed him. He wanted to fuck. He wanted to make love. He wanted Dylan inside him. Around him. Over him. He wanted it all and it scared him. He just didn't have the words to admit any of it. Suddenly, shy and pissed at himself, he clambered off of Dylan and stood up. A head rush kept him immobile for a second or two, enough time for Dylan to stand as well. There was no expression on Dylan's face, well, nothing Lucas could get his head around. If anything, Dylan looked wary and a little concerned.

"It's okay. Sorry. Being stupid." Lucas stumbled over the words and took one step away and then another until he was walking back through the trees in the general direction of the hotel. *Shit. Balls.* He'd just embarrassed himself with the hot beach bum-waiter-barman-photographer.

"Wait," Dylan called. Lucas just hurried his steps, but then with an oomph, found himself spun around and pinned to a tree by a scowling Dylan. "Don't walk off."

"Let me go."

"I'm not letting you go." As if to emphasize the point, Dylan pressed against him and Lucas very quickly became aware of just how hard Dylan was. "What happened there? You didn't even let me answer?"

"I don't want you to feel you have to do anything you don't want to." Experimentally, he pushed against Dylan, but all that did was align their dicks so that he got the delicious friction of a solid body against his. If anything, he was harder and needier than he had been on the sand.

"Does it feel like I don't want you?" Dylan murmured. "You are the most gorgeous, sexy, complicated, sad guy I have ever met." He paused and moved to slide their cloth-covered dicks against each other. Lucas couldn't stop the near whimper that left his mouth. "I want nothing more than to spread you out on a bed and taste you from head to toe. But—" Again, he stopped and began to move more insistently. Each thrust was a delicious press of flesh and Lucas unconsciously matched the movement until they were literally bringing each other off just through touch alone. "—I only have half an hour and I want all night with you."

Dylan finished talking and captured Lucas's lips in a heated kiss. Tongues dueled for dominance and memories flooded Lucas of what it was like to be pinned and held and forced to feel by an experienced lover. It had been far too long. He blindly gripped Dylan, and helpless to move, simply held on for the ride. People were no more than twenty feet away and the only thing that stopped them from seeing were the trees. The extra frisson of excitement curled into an orgasm that built at the base of his spine and in his balls. So long. It had been so long. Pushing away the pain in his stomach, he concentrated on nothing more than the scent and taste of this man.

"Lucas…" Dylan murmured in his ear. His voice dripped with want and an answering need for more awoke inside Lucas. "So gorgeous. Want you so much… so fucking much. The taste of you." Dylan kept talking, a litany of praise and encouragement. When he slid a hand inside the material of Lucas's shorts and closed it around Lucas, just the touch of his confident fingers took Lucas to the peak.

He lost it so fast he couldn't say a word; he simply leaned his head back against the trunk of the tree and repeated one word over and over. "Fuck."

Dylan took a step away and Lucas felt the loss keenly. But when Dylan pressed a single hand against the trunk beside him and then used the hand wet with Lucas's come to ease his own erection to orgasm, Lucas went weak at the knees. That was possibly, no, definitely the most erotic thing he had ever seen. When Dylan had held his gaze and lost himself to orgasm, Lucas didn't think he had ever seen anything so damn perfect.

"Happy birthday," Lucas said. Dylan smiled, and having finished, they held each other close for a second.

"I want more than just that with you," Dylan whispered.

More? Lucas thought. More might just kill him.

Chapter Eight

"What's up with you?"

Lucas raised an eyebrow and looked at his sister over the top of his shades. "What's up with me?" He was perfectly happy. "What's up with you?"

"Nothing," Tasha claimed and sat up on the lounger to stare at the pool.

Lucas sighed and folded his arms across his chest. "You've been married five days and you're sitting by the pool with your brother. What's wrong with this picture?"

Raising her leg, Tasha rested her chin on her knee and tilted her head to look at Lucas. "I'm fine. Mike and Olly organized a fishing trip with the hotel guys. Dylan and Scott?"

Lucas smiled at the mention of Dylan's name and even felt okay knowing he was out to sea with the other barman, Scott. Only yesterday he'd revealed to Dylan that he was a little jealous of Scott, all tall and tanned and far too sexy for his own good. *"Scott? He's a friend. It's only his first year here. I like him but I don't want to sleep with him."*

Lucas smiled at the memory and then pulled himself back to Tasha.

"So, Liam ditched you for a boys' day out," he stated. "You could have gone too."

Tasha pulled such a face that Lucas didn't even want to guess what it meant. "I don't like fish." When they were kids, their parents had taken them on a fishing trip. Lucas had caught one and had tormented his sister by chasing her around the boat for about ten minutes. The fish had been tiny. Strangely, since then, Tasha had had a thing about fish. "They're all wet and slimy and have these beady eyes," she continued. "Plus, the idiots are going looking for sharks. I swear to God, if they let my husband get eaten by some fucking shark, I will kill them."

Though he knew he shouldn't, Lucas couldn't help but laugh. Tasha cursed pretty much never. "They'll be fine. Liam will be fine." He tried to sound reassuring. "It's not like they went out alone. Dylan will keep them safe." Dylan certainly had made him feel safe on more than one occasion. Over the last few days, they had ventured out onto and into the water, and not once had Lucas felt wary or concerned. For once, he'd been completely at ease and able to relax, knowing Dylan was there with him. The ocean was a beautiful place and he was glad to finally be able to explore it with someone so passionate about the deep blue haven. Dylan was young and exciting, and it had been a long time since Lucas had felt so alive.

Tasha pressed her mouth in a thoughtful line. "Dylan," she said with a sigh. "I hear you've been spending quite a bit of time with him."

She'd heard? Who the hell from? Like he really needed

to ask. He and Dylan had bumped into Kate and her husband, Mike, a couple of times in the last few days. It had nothing to do with her what he did with his time. In fact, it was nobody's business but his how and with whom he spent his vacation.

"Well? You going to tell me? Because, between you and me, you look a hell of a lot better since we got out here, and I think maybe a certain captain has had something to do with that." She met his eyes through his shades and he could feel the heat of embarrassment rising from his neck. A grin quickly spread across her face. "I knew it. You're so obvious."

What did she want him to say? "Sure, I've been spending some time with him. He's an interesting man." He wasn't sure he was up to a heart to heart with his baby sister about exactly how Dylan made him feel. "And I know it's hard to believe, but I've actually been enjoying myself." He had. He really had. Lucas glanced to where his cell phone was sitting on a table between them. Maybe he'd had too much fun. Municipal hadn't yet been in contact, but he knew it was only a matter of time. The contract was still sitting in the safe in his room and they'd want to check on his progress. There was an influx of guilt in his stomach as he thought about all the hard work Alan had put into the document prior to his death. Even if both of them had been looking to move on, Alan would never have left Municipal on a half-assed job.

"You seeing him tonight?" Tasha cut into his thoughts with the question.

"Erm, I dunno." They hadn't really been making any plans, just going day to day grabbing moments here and there. Lucas, after all, was the one on vacation, not Dylan. Along with Scott, Dylan was involved with the running of excursions for the guests. Lucas had joined the group for one trip to Marsh Harbor. But amid the flurry of activity and people in the town, all he wanted was to return to the Cay. To be honest, he'd thought he was going to have a full-blown panic attack in the street. Luckily, Dylan had sensed something wasn't quite right, and had guided him in the direction of a bar. How the fuck was he going to cope going back to the city?

"Earth to Luc."

"Hmm?" He looked at his sister. "What?" Had she said something?

"I said, do you want to come and see the honeymoon cabin tonight? We've arranged for a barbeque on the terrace, so you could join us for something to eat. Maybe if Dylan's free you could bring him along."

Lucas gave a nervous laugh. That would be just great. He'd rather toss himself on the grill than watch the painful roasting of Dylan by Tasha about his intentions towards her brother. "I dunno, Tash." This was riskily edging into date territory.

Getting to her feet, Tasha released the towel wrapped around her chest. Her skin already had a healthy glow and he smiled as she stepped from under the large parasol and the tan lines from the straps of one of her other bikinis became more obvious in the sunlight. "Ask him, or I will," she said with a smirk and headed to the side of the pool. Delicately, she tested the temperature with her toe before stepping down into water and disappearing beneath the surface.

Did he have the courage to ask? Lucas glanced back at his cell phone. Did he have the time? He really needed to get in a day of work. He chewed on his lip as he considered Tasha's invitation that had turned into an almost-threat. There were still a few days to the deadline. He had plenty of time.

"THAT WASN'T SO BAD," DYLAN SAID, WRAPPING HIS HAND in Lucas's as they headed back along the beach.

When Lucas had asked him out for the evening, Dylan had gotten the impression Lucas was not really looking forward to it. Okay, so Tasha had been straight there with the interrogation, but Dylan hadn't expected anything less. It was clear the siblings cared a lot about each other. He knew they'd only had each other for a long time.

"I guess," Lucas said as he linked his fingers with Dylan's in a loose hold. Slowly, he swung their arms and guided Dylan down to the water's edge. "I'm sorry if you felt uncomfortable. Tash can be a little intense."

"Only because she cares about you," Dylan added. Sometimes Dylan wished he'd had someone, a brother or sister, to share his grief. Reaching out, he took Lucas's other hand and, with a smile, pulled Lucas toward him for a kiss. "You're lucky to have her." He locked lips with Lucas, taking his time to taste and tease Lucas's mouth.

"I'm lucky to have you," Lucas said and pulled back, clearly surprised by his admission. "Sorry. That came out wrong."

Dylan raised a hand to Lucas's face and tenderly

cupped his jaw. "No." He shook his head. "That came out just right." He smiled and pulled Lucas into a hug. It had been a long time since he'd felt wanted in the way Lucas wanted him. Despite everything, he missed having someone to call family, lover. Damn, heat shot to the head of his dick and all he could do was think about how much he wanted to make love to the man. He hadn't yet managed to have the night he wanted with Lucas. The opportunity just hadn't arisen—until now. Seeking out Lucas's mouth, he teased his lips into a kiss, sucking and biting as he held onto the only person who mattered right then. "I wanna," he said breathlessly between heavy kisses. "I wanna have you. I want you."

The three beers from that evening spurred him on. He wanted Lucas and he knew Lucas wanted him just as badly. Now was their chance. He just had to get Lucas off the damn beach and into his bed.

"Mine," Lucas uttered and forcefully broke the kiss. His eyes were wide and his cheeks flushed as he stared at Dylan in the evening light. He twisted his hand in the material of Dylan's shirt and caught his breath. "Mine," he said again.

Dylan nodded. "I know a shortcut." He grabbed Lucas by the hand, guiding him up the beach and steering them between the line of trees at the edge of the sand. He'd happily fuck Lucas right here and now, but as was his way, he hadn't thought that far ahead. They walked quickly, ducking as they made their way through the overgrown diversion. Lucas's hand tightened around his. "Don't worry. I know this place like the back of my hand." He darted to the left, pulling Lucas with him. Maybe he seemed a little too keen, but fuck if he hadn't been thinking about this since they first kissed. He wanted Lucas like he'd never wanted anyone before.

The next few minutes were the longest of his life. His whole body ached with anticipation. He was hard and Lucas knew it. He pressed his body against Lucas's as they stood outside his room. He ran his hand over Lucas's ass as he waited for him to unlock the door. What the hell was taking so long?

"Fuck," Lucas hissed as he pushed at the handle. "Damn thing keeps sticking—" He didn't even finish before the door came unstuck, opening and causing him to half fall into his room.

Dylan laughed as he pulled the keys from the lock and pushed the door closed behind them. Securing the door, he turned and looked at Lucas. His erection pushed at the front of his pants and he wanted nothing more than to fuck Lucas into next week and back again. Crossing the room, he began to unbutton his shirt and met Lucas in a messy embrace and sloppy kiss. In a few clumsy moves they were both stripped naked and falling in a tangle of limbs onto the bed. God, he needed this. Rolling them over, he managed to position himself over Lucas's thighs. He wrapped his hand around Lucas's wrists and pressed them in the soft bedding above his head.

"So hot," he said and leaned over Lucas, trailing a line of kisses across his collarbone and upward to meet his mouth. "You really are." Releasing Lucas's hands, Dylan carefully slid down Lucas's legs and hooked an arm under each of Lucas's knees. Lifting Lucas's legs from the bed, he moved into the space he created, lying on the bed as he circled Lucas's dick with his mouth. He smiled around the erection as Lucas arched off the bed and let out a soft groan. It was a magnificent sound and he gently lifted Lucas's legs higher over his shoulders, creating an angle that had Lucas pushed down on the bed.

With slow movements, he gradually drew Lucas's full length between his lips. Teasing and sucking, he applied pressure to his balls and then circled his hands under Lucas's ass, urging him to fuck upward into his mouth. Sharp thrusts into Dylan's mouth had Lucas moaning that he was close within a few minutes and Dylan sucked hard one more time, not wanting to tip him over just yet. With a grin, he released Lucas's dick.

Shuddering with pleasure, Lucas pawed above his head, desperately reaching for the drawer beside the bed. With a grunt, he fell back on the covers. "Fuck," he said and breathed in deeply. "Want you in me."

Dylan teasingly ran his tongue over the length of Lucas's erection before sliding his arms from under Lucas's legs and crawling upward. Kissing Lucas, he reached over Lucas's head for the drawer. He lifted his head and found the condom and lube Lucas had been searching for. Coating his fingers, he then distracted Lucas with more kisses as he slid his hand between Lucas's legs. Tenderly, he stroked the back of his hand over the inside of Lucas's thigh before heading south. As he pushed inside, Lucas deepened the kiss and swept his tongue across Dylan's, and Dylan thought it was the hottest thing ever. He savored the moment, enjoying Lucas tasting and damn near fucking every inch of his mouth with his tongue. His dick was hard and Christ he needed to be in Lucas already.

Finding some focus, he finished his preparation and quickly fumbled to put on the condom.

"From behind," Lucas said as he sat forward and turned onto his knees. Dylan didn't really care right now, front, back, hanging from the fucking ceiling, he'd fuck Lucas any way he could.

"Okay," Dylan agreed and got up on his knees, positioning himself behind Lucas. *Christ.* He caught sight of Lucas spreading himself open, inviting him inside, and he thought he was going to come right then and there. Whatever Lucas might think of himself, Dylan thought he was beyond gorgeous and definitely hot as fuck laid out and ready for him. Kneeling between Lucas's legs, he guided himself forward, teasing Lucas for a moment as he ran the head of his dick up and down the crease of Lucas's ass. God. No more teasing. The sensation was driving him crazy. Steadying himself, he held onto Lucas's hip and rocked forward.

"Oh God," Lucas groaned.

Dylan thought the exact same thing as he pushed into the tight heat of Lucas's body. Holding on with both hands, he began a slow fuck forward until he was balls deep. A few firm, deep thrusts and he set a rhythm. Sounds rolled off Lucas's tongue and Dylan was right there with him, fucking himself to a climax. After agonizing minutes of teetering on the edge of orgasm, he fell over the edge and into blissful release.

"Fuck," he whimpered as he held on tight to Lucas. "Holy fuck." Panting, he collapsed across Lucas's back and squirmed as Lucas continued to gently rock beneath him. Reaching around and beneath Lucas, he gave a few quick tugs of Lucas's dick until the man was coming right there with him and they collapsed in a sticky mess onto the bed. He planted heavy kisses to Lucas's sweat-slicked back before pulling out and rolling away.

They lay there for a little while simply looking into each other's eyes as they caught their breath. Smiling, Dylan edged closer and snuggled his head into the crease of Lucas's bent arm. Gently, he stroked his fingertips up and down Lucas's spine, smiling as he saw the goose pimples rise across Lucas's skin in a delightful shudder. He wanted to say something, but right now he wasn't sure he could string together a sentence that wouldn't come across as ridiculous. Silence was his friend, he decided. Instead, he continued to touch and stroke Lucas's heated skin, hugging him close.

Eventually, the need to move overwhelmed him, and he reluctantly sat up. He was surprised when Lucas's caught his wrist. Meeting Lucas's eyes, he realized there was fear in them, fear he was leaving. With a smile, he leaned down and kissed Lucas on the cheek. "Bathroom," he said before sliding from Lucas's hold and heading across the room.

"Will you stay?" Lucas asked as they returned to bed.

Dylan lay on the pillow beside Lucas and smiled reassuringly. "Of course. I said I wanted a whole night, remember?" He never wanted it to be a quick fuck and then leave.

Lucas nodded and let out a sigh.

"What?" Dylan said. Obviously, something was bothering Lucas.

"I was just thinking about next week. When I leave."

"You shouldn't think about it, not yet anyway. You have seven glorious days left on the island. Enjoy them." Dylan understood exactly how Lucas felt. The island was like a whole other world where anything seemed possible. Nothing could bother them out there. Sapphire Cay was a place of dreams. It touched people in ways they couldn't imagine.

Lucas rolled onto his back and stared up at the ceiling fan. "Where will you go next month?"

He didn't want to think past the end of tonight at the moment, let alone a few weeks down the line. "I was thinking about moving on to a hotel in Los Angeles; they always have work for me and I miss the worst of hurricane season here. Thing is, I had a different kind of offer and I thought maybe it wasn't for me, but I'm starting to reconsider."

"Offer?" Lucas's interest was piqued. "What kind?"

Should I say? "Sapphire Cay." There was a strange silence between them, and Dylan met Lucas's interested eyes. "What?"

"You? They offered you the island?"

Okay, Lucas sounded a little too astonished. "Sure, why wouldn't they?"

Lucas shook his head. "Oh, no, I didn't mean… I'm just a little surprised. You follow the sun, right?" He repeated Dylan's mantra and reached out to gently circle the sun on his wrist. Lucas's touch was warm and comforting as he traced the tattooed line of text.

"I also said some things were worth settling down for if you did it for the right reasons." *Sapphire Cay was a damn good reason.* "I've been traveling a long time now, and the benefits of moving on again this year no longer outweigh the benefits of committing here." He'd been traveling the globe for years and not one place had felt as much like home as the Cay had. It was beautiful, and because of it, he had met some equally beautiful people.

"Can you afford it?" Lucas gave him a curious look.

Laughing, Dylan said, "Yeah, I can afford it." Maybe this was what his mother's money had always been meant for. Mitch Stone had said she would want him to be happy. The island and its staff and visitors certainly did that. "It's just an idea." He'd told Jeanie he had money in a trust the first year he'd been here. Money that was for him to make a life for himself. He'd not touched it yet—hadn't really wanted it—but this time things felt different. Maybe he had finally outrun the need to live life only for today. He'd been ill for so long, and after four years of treatment for lymphoma and staring at hospital walls, a failed attempt at settling into a normal life, a job, and a relationship with a guy just like his father, the call of freedom and space had been too loud. Now though, with his birthday and the money, it seemed he was ready to stop running.

"It's a great idea," Lucas agreed and he gave the impression he meant it.

"Maybe. Antoine and Jeanie make it look easy, but working here and actually owning and running the place are two vastly different things. Could you really see me greeting guests and being the face of Sapphire Cay?"

Lucas lifted his head from the pillow and leaned forward, giving Dylan a tender kiss. "I'm pretty sure you could do anything you put your mind to." He smiled and gently rested his hand on Dylan's chest. "You should seriously consider it." Lucas closed his eyes and snuggled in close. "You really should," he said again. He sounded tired.

Dylan slowly stroked his hand through Lucas's hair as he considered the offer. Could he really run something like this? He was more about the hands-on and doing side of things. Give him a hammer and some nails or a boat to drive and he was happy. Running a business and doing accounts, wages, orders, could he handle that? There was only one thing for it. Closing his eyes and resting his forehead against Lucas's, he whispered, "Would you stay here with me?" When he got no answer, he opened his eyes. Smiling, he gently laid a kiss on the sleeping man's cheek. It was probably for the best. He had no idea what he would have done if Lucas had said yes.

Chapter Nine

When Dylan caught his reflection in his closet mirror, he wondered for a few seconds if he should be dressing up for this meeting. Maybe he should go back into the main room and wake Lucas up, get him to pass over neat pants and a shirt. Dylan grimaced at the thought. He even considered wearing his black jeans and white shirt from the bar, but it screamed 'work-Dylan'. Antoine and Jeanie thought he was good enough and they had seen him in swim trunks more often than not. Smart jeans and his cleanest, tidiest T-shirt were going to be a huge improvement on that at least.

Grabbing his notebook and smoothing the cover, he stood for a few moments at the bedroom door and looked in at Lucas. Just watching him sprawled on the bed under the lazily turning ceiling fan was enough to make him grin like an idiot. The last few days in a row they had ended up back here in Dylan's small two-room cabin and slept the entire night. A sense of peace washed over Dylan when Lucas stirred in his sleep and moved into the space that

Dylan had left only a short while before. Lucas was a mattress stealer of epic proportions and the only way to keep him still in his sometimes troubled sleep was to wrap his arms around Lucas and hold him close. Proximity and the firm hold settled Lucas more than anything else. Not for the first time Dylan wondered what the hell was going on in Lucas's head; so often his face was creased in a frown.

Pulling his gaze away from the sleeping man, Dylan made his way out of the cabin and through the trees to the main reception area. He had asked for this breakfast meeting with Antoine and Jeanie, but he was nervous enough to just jump back in bed. He needed a shot of caffeine but the thought of food just churned in his stomach. Jeanie offered him breakfast but Dylan refused and instead slid into the spare seat opposite his two friends.

"Is everything okay?" she asked. She looked concerned and kept looking at Antoine, who concentrated hard on the eggs on his plate. Antoine clearly thought he knew what was coming. Every year for the last five years, he had met them at this table to explain why he was leaving and why it was important that he went. Every year, they smiled and accepted he was happy with his life—however many times Antoine said he wanted Dylan to stay. This year was different. If they found a buyer for Sapphire Cay then there would be no more breakfasts together, not like this, and maybe Dylan would lose the place he had begun to think of as his home, his place of safety.

Putting the notebook full of his ideas on the table, he inhaled a breath of courage and began.

"I wanted to talk to you about the island. I have the financing in place and I want to revisit the idea of me buying it." Aware he had blurted everything out in a not-entirely professional way, he winced. What were they going to say? Had he left it too long to say yes?

Tears filled Jeanie's eyes and she reached a hand across the table to cover his. He felt emotion choke his throat. They would know how hard this was for him and what thought processes he had gone through to get to this point. Even Antoine looked up from his eggs with an expression of shock on his face.

"That is wonderful news," Antoine finally said. He laid down his knife and fork, and for a second they sat in silence. Then Dylan used his free hand to open the notebook to page one.

"I had some thoughts."

DYLAN FELT DRAINED. TWO HOURS THEY HAD SAT AT THE table and talked and everything had been so official. They only stopped discussions when the first of the wedding guests made their way to breakfast.

Seeing the guests made everything even more official, wrapped up in permanent. This time next year it would be him responsible for these people, for the island, for everything. Tension knotted in his forehead and he pressed at the sharp pain. Doing this, investing in the Cay, was the closest he would come to perpetually stopping anywhere. Grabbing a tray of hot food and rolls, large glasses of orange juice, and two containers of coffee, he made his way back to the cabin hoping he wouldn't meet Lucas on the way up to find him. He had things he needed to think about but he needed to give himself a break. What better place to forget everything for a while than eating breakfast with his lover?

"Coffee?" Dylan waved the caffeine near Lucas's face and swore he had never seen anything cuter than Lucas blearily opening his eyes and yawning.

"I'm dead," Lucas muttered.

"Wake up, I have coffee, breakfast."

"You killed me with sex," Lucas added. At least he kept his eyes open, and Dylan dropped a small kiss on his forehead.

"Nah, killed by love," Dylan said simply. He immediately regretted saying that when Lucas's eyes widened comically. He'd just used the 'L word' without even realizing it.

"Anyway," he changed the subject. "Coffee. Up and at 'em."

"Whattimeizzit?" Lucas slurred and stretched tall in the bed, grabbing the bars of the headboard and extending each muscle before relaxing. His morning wood was insistently up and awake against his belly, and his skin had lost that sickly paleness he had arrived with and was now glowing with warmth and color. Dylan was looking at the sexiest man he had ever seen. When Lucas grinned and shuffled to sit upright to take the coffee, Dylan had to stop himself from pushing the caffeine to one side and climbing back into bed with Lucas.

Instead, he sat himself on the chair next to the bed and propped his legs up on the mattress. Together they cleared off the eggs, bacon, and the biscuits, all while Lucas lay naked and hard on the bed. Dylan didn't know how he was keeping himself from simply jumping Lucas and wondered if this was it. *I decide to buy an island and lose my sex drive. Great.*

"How long have you been up?" Lucas asked on another yawn. He was adorably rumpled and sleepy, a sight Dylan could get used to.

"Couple of hours; had a meeting with Antoine and Jeanie."

"Are you free the rest of the morning?"

"Until eleven."

Lucas glanced up at the small clock on the wall and then back at Dylan.

"Come back to bed then?"

There was nothing Dylan would like to do more, but he had to get some things out in the open before he exploded with the nervous tension inside him.

"We will but can I ask you something first…?" His voice trailed away. Asking Lucas for help was like deciding he was definitely handing over money and buying a freaking island. Lucas raised his eyebrows in reaction to serious-Dylan, but he evidently picked up on the change in tone and sat up cross-legged in front of Dylan.

"Is something wrong?" he asked, concerned.

"Not wrong exactly. I just have this thing and I wondered if you could look at it for me."

Lucas waggled his eyebrows lewdly. "I'll be happy to look at your thing," he said.

"I told Antoine and Jeanie that I was interested in buying the island from them, and they have this contract they want me to look at, like a draft thing. They also want me to sign a proviso that their son Jamie can come onto the island gratis to do work. I mean that sounds like a good idea, but I've never met him, and it would be my island I guess—"

"You really do have seven hundred thousand dollars?" There was a lot of emphasis on the 'do' and Dylan hesitated. Did Lucas think he had been joking when he had told him he could afford it? And why focus on that when Dylan had so many other things he wanted to discuss? He clammed up and dropped his feet to the floor. Maybe now was not a good time to talk if Lucas wasn't going to take him seriously.

"When I was born, my mom died because of complications of preeclampsia. I never knew her."

"I'm sorry, Dylan."

"It is what it is," Dylan said softly. He shrugged, refusing to let himself go down the path of self-pity or one that meant Lucas felt sorry for him. He still had a lot more to say. "I have this money that my dad invested for me, her money. I want to use it to make something new for me."

"That sounds like a good idea—"

"That isn't everything though. I didn't want the money. I wanted a mom. And I wanted a dad who wasn't bitter and buried in work. When I was seven I was diagnosed with lymphoma. Four years of treatment and dad tried. But hell, he was losing his only child like he had lost his wife. We were never close even after I got the all-clear."

"Shit, Dylan. I'm so sorry."

"You don't need to be sorry—"

"That explains the need to follow the sun," Lucas

interrupted. His voice was soft but it didn't hold pity; it held understanding.

"Yes." Dylan wasn't going to lie. "So yes, I do have money. Money that my dad looked after and thinks is the answer to everything—even grief. But I want to do something with it, for myself and for Jeanie and Antoine, and for Scott and the chef and hell, I want to create a family here. I want you to understand that I am taking this seriously." Dylan pasted his serious expression on in the hope it hid his uncertainty.

"Sorry. Look, I'm sorry. I do understand." Lucas scrambled to stand. Apparently, Dylan wasn't hiding his emotions well enough. "Shit, let me get a shower and some clothes then I'll get into contract mode and we'll talk."

"You don't think less of me? Or mind helping?" Dylan hated the edge of pleading in his voice. He wasn't used to being in a position where he wanted to ask for help, understanding, or advice from anyone. He had made his own way to this point in his life.

"Of course I don't mind," Lucas said. "This sounds like the perfect idea for you."

Dylan wished he felt as confident as Lucas sounded.

LUCAS QUICKLY SHOWERED AND DRESSED WHILE contemplating the solemn expression on Dylan's face. He was deadly serious about this island-buying and Lucas knew, without being arrogant, that he was the best person to help the man out. They wouldn't be at contract stage yet, but he could at least give Dylan some kind of heads-up on what to look out for.

"There's quite a lot of behind-the-scenes repairs to do. Then I have these ideas: a Jacuzzi in the honeymoon cabin, maybe some improvements to the main restaurant—"

"Slow down," Lucas said. His words were gentle. "Let's focus on the proposal Antoine and Jeanie gave you. It seems fair; clearly there are the whole land registration issues—you'll need to get a lawyer involved in that—but if you are happy, is it a fair price?"

"I think it is. I know it is."

"Have you thought about income? Will you have money left to support a quiet season? You'll need to renew the insurances, get them in your name." Lucas couldn't believe the excitement building inside him as he considered the possibilities for Dylan. This excitement was the part of contract management that had long since been drummed out of him at Municipal. There it was all profit, margin, steal. Nothing like the challenge of something new. Maybe Dylan wouldn't mind if he dipped in and out of this new world Dylan was creating, give him help if it was needed. Lucas considered whether Dylan would contact him in the future if he had questions. He may well live in Seattle, the furthest point away in the northwest, but there were still email and cell phones. Emotion stole his breath, a wash of disappointment and jealousy when his brain reminded him: it's a holiday fling, it's just sex. He won't need you after this week is up.

Dylan would find a business manager in the Bahamas, maybe up in the US in Miami instead. Lucas was, for all intents and purposes, removing himself from the situation as soon as he left Sapphire Cay. Why did that thought create so much jealousy inside him? He blamed Dylan. Dylan had been the one to say they were making love, not having sex, and that single statement had initiated the fear that now curled in his belly. Fear that loving Dylan would mean he had to give up on his well-thought-out and meticulously planned future. But what if he came back to Sapphire Cay? What if he went home, handed in his notice, cashed in everything, and brought his tired and ill body back down to the Cay? Would losing the stress of eighteen-hour days mean his ulcers would go? That his blood pressure would return to normal? Would it mean he could stop taking pills for uppers and meds as downers? Could he get a handle on his life?

Fuck. Would Dylan even want him after the week was up?

"Earth to Lucas," Dylan said loudly. Lucas snapped out of his thoughts to see a smiling Dylan waving a hand in front of his face, and he pushed aside the doubts and self-defeating thoughts. This wasn't about him. This was about the young man who had his whole life ahead of him and had just found some new purpose in his existence. So why was he identifying Dylan as young and why did he suddenly feel so old?

"Sorry?"

Dylan pulled the papers from Lucas's hand and pushed him back on the bed to straddle his lap. With a smile he leaned down and kissed Lucas lightly before deepening the kiss with an appreciative groan. Lucas forgot all his thoughts of being old and having no part of Dylan's life and simply lost himself to the kiss. They only had a few days left and he was going to make the most of them.

———

Tasha caught up with Lucas on the beach.

"Packed?" she asked as she sat down next to him, cross-legged.

"Nearly," he answered. Lying back on the soft sand, he stared up at the cloudless blue and tried to commit to memory the scents and sounds of the island, storing them up for times when this was all over.

"I don't really want to leave," she said. "It's been so unreal."

I know the feeling, Lucas thought. He didn't say the words aloud though—she didn't need to know how he was feeling. He'd finished his last job for Municipal, although they didn't know it yet. He'd made sure the work Alan started was complete to the best of his ability and had used the hotel office fax to send the papers to Oscar Morgan at the head office. That had been three days before and since then everything had been a blur of desperately wanting to enjoy the last few days he had with Dylan, but also getting his head around facing what he had to do in Seattle.

This wasn't his time to talk about how he was going to be missing Dylan and the island so much it was like he was preparing to have a limb removed. Instead, he changed the subject as cleverly as he could manage given how lethargic he was feeling in the shade of the trees.

"Where's your husband?" he asked.

Tasha snorted a laugh. "Liam's around somewhere

with Dylan and Scott doing man stuff. They're comparing boat sizes or something equally 'manly'."

Lucas chuckled. Liam had spent so much time out on the water that Lucas wondered how his new brother-in-law would manage the cold waters of the Chesapeake near their new home. Not exactly the Bahamian waters even on a good day.

"Thank you, Lucas," Tasha said.

"What for?" Lucas was puzzled at first, thinking back on the short conversation they had just had and wondering if he had missed anything.

"For the years since we lost Mom and Dad. For not giving up on your teenage sister. For making me get my degree. Hell, working yourself into the ground so that you could pay for it all. For helping organize my beautiful wedding and for welcoming Liam into our small family."

Lucas was quiet for a second. That was a long list of thank yous to get his head around. He and Tasha were close; she was his only family and he would do anything for her. There was no question of choosing to ensure she was happy. It was his job.

"You're welcome, sis," he finally said. Tasha huffed a laugh and then lay back to join him in staring up at the sky. She reached for his hand and held it tight. The act reminded Lucas of so many nights where they had fallen asleep in the same room, where he was the big brother and he looked after his sister. Every single second together had made them closer than most of his friends were with their siblings. He would miss her when she moved to Washington for Liam's work.

"You can stop now though."

The words hung in the air and a crazy mix of pride and grief curled in Lucas. He wasn't going to ask what she meant. He knew. She was telling him that he could rely on Liam to look after her and that it was his time to *be*.

"Thank you," he said simply. She squeezed his hand and they didn't say anything else. Something cracked around his heart, a barrier, a protection, and instead he was flooded with certainty. Yes, it was his time to find his own path, away from his self-imposed expectations and rules. Now was the time for him to take chances.

"Is this a private party?" Liam said as he slumped down on the sand next to them. This time it was Lucas's turn to squeeze Tasha's hand. They had little more than an hour before the boat took them back to the mainland and Tasha and her new husband, the man who was her new life, should have the time on their own. Lucas rolled to stand and brushed off sand, ignoring the head rush and the accompanying pain deep in his gut.

"I need to finish packing. See you at the boat in an hour." Then with a final smile down at the happy couple, he went back to his cabin.

There was evidence of Dylan there. They had alternated between his place and Dylan's place, and Dylan had left a toothbrush, a jacket, a pair of cutoff jeans. Then there was the scent of him.

Pushing the last of his things into the suitcase, Lucas zipped it shut. Casting an eye around to check for anything he missed, he picked up the shower gel that Dylan used and hoped it wasn't going to be viewed as too creepy when he unzipped his case a bit and pushed the plastic bottle deep inside. Seattle was a cold dark gray cloud on his horizon and the nebulous idea of capturing Dylan's sunshine made him start to doubt his own sanity.

"Ready?" Lucas turned quickly to see Dylan leaning against the doorjamb.

How long had he been standing there? Had Dylan seen him hide the gel away, literally steal the gel? Embarrassment flooded him momentarily and he dropped his gaze.

"As I'll ever be," he mumbled. He concentrated on the case and fiddled with the zipper as if it were the most important thing he had to do right now. Far more important than falling into Dylan's arms and holding him close.

"I wish you didn't have to go," Dylan said. His voice was soft and he moved away from the door to stand right next to Lucas.

"Real life calls." Lucas sighed. He looked up as he spoke and couldn't fail to see the flash of hurt in Dylan's expression. "I mean… I can't stay on an island for the rest of my life… I have work. I didn't mean that life was any more real than this…"

"Shhhh," Dylan muttered. "No more talking." They gravitated to a close hug and neither man spoke. Lucas forced down the words that threatened to spill from his lips. *I want to stay. I love you.* What could he give Dylan now? A man who didn't even know his own path?

"Not talking," he mumbled against warm skin. Those were the only words he allowed out.

"Promise me something," Dylan asked. "Know that anytime you need somewhere to come to get out of the city, to relax, you come here. Promise me?"

Lucas closed his eyes and buried his face in the

juncture of Dylan's neck and shoulder, against the solid presence of the man who would be holding his heart after he left.

"I promise," he said. Emotion choked him and he was lucky he managed those two words.

The hour passed quickly and before Lucas knew it, he was seated in the boat heading for the mainland.

Reaching their destination, Dylan expertly steered the small boat into the harbor and began to assist in unloading bags. Lucas was lost in his own thoughts but his sister interrupted him with a loud whisper.

"Don't be stupid. Stay here. Go back with Dylan."

He couldn't answer. He had genuine responsibilities and things to do with a capital T.

Dylan would know what Lucas had to do. Dylan understood. Then maybe, just maybe, Lucas could make those first steps to restart his life.

Chapter Ten

"As always, a job well done."

Lucas did his best to look positive as Oscar Morgan wrapped a strong hand around his and gave it a firm shake.

"Knew we could count on you to wade through all the bullcrap and get the contracts signed and sealed." Oscar released Lucas's hand and sat back in his chair. "You did a good job digging Patterson out of a hole." He gave a crooked smile as he added, "I decided we could maybe groom him a little more, so we're not dismissing him, just moving him across to our North Carolina office. He'll be better suited there."

Lucas gave a slow nod. It could have been worse for the kid. "Thank you." The praise should have been enough to lift Lucas's mood. But instead, all it did was draw upon his deepest fears. He was about to do something that only a year ago he would never have imagined. He was going to resign.

"You wanted to talk to me." Oscar looked at him from beneath his creased, dark brow. *Did he suspect?*

This was where Lucas was supposed to reach into his jacket and pull out the printed and signed letter of resignation. He'd spent the last week finding just the right words. His first attempt had been a flurry of angry and sad words all mixed up in some weird mess of guilt and blame on Municipal's part for the death of his friend and the slow murder of his own soul. Obviously, that wasn't quite what was done in this corporate world. So, over time, the words formed into what was needed. Thanks for the years and faith in his ability, but it was time to move on to pastures new and some other equally contrived garbage.

Well, here went nothing. "Oscar, I've been having some doubts, I suppose, about my position here—"

"It's yours."

"What?"

"The West Coast and the Delaney contract. It's all yours."

Well, fuck. He had always been considered the natural choice after Alan, but with Patterson being brought in, he just assumed Morgan wanted to split the region and keep Lucas where he was, doing what he did, and doing it well.

"Delaney?" That was a multimillion-dollar venture, the bonus alone could... Hell, he could buy his own freaking island right next door to Sapphire Cay.

Oscar nodded. "Thinking Patterson could be better than you in any way was a mistake. I guess it was selfishness on my own part. You're a damn good manager."

This was some kind of joke, right? Why now? He had made a decision after finally getting his head around his options. "Thank you. I don't know what to say."

"Well, yes would be a good start." There was a peculiar look in Oscar's eyes, one of disbelief and impatience. He obviously thought Lucas should have jumped at the offer, and under normal circumstances, Lucas would have.

Lucas pressed his lips in a line. This was what he had been working for all these years. The reason he had worked every hour he could, the reason he hadn't had a decent relationship in years, and the reason his body ached and he was popping more meds than a supermodel on diet pills.

"I need to think about it," he said, and straightaway he sensed the temperature in the room drop. He met Oscar's cool stare but somehow held his ground. He just needed a moment. This was big. This was what he'd given ten years of his life for.

"If that's what you want," Oscar said and rested his elbows on the edge of his desk as he pressed the palms of his hands together. He looked at Lucas as if he were trying to figure out what it was that had Lucas shying away from the offer. "But this is the only offer on the table right now. There will be no budging on our end."

"Of course." He got to his feet and pressed his hand to his breast pocket as he turned on his heel and left Oscar's office. The lump of the folded envelope was still there like some kind of security blanket. He should just pull it out and throw it at Oscar and then run for the hills. That wouldn't exactly be the grownup thing to do. He smiled to himself. Sapphire Cay had renewed the youthful mischief in him, he figured.

Running a hand back through his freshly trimmed hair,

he made his way past the line of cubicles to his own office at the end of the row. As he stepped inside, he was surprised to find Rosemary Johnson sitting at his desk.

"Rosemary," he said, "how lovely to see you."

Rosemary looked her usual stunning self. Her dark hair had been swept back from her face and pinned high on her head, her makeup was flawless, and her figure-hugging red coat accentuated her feminine curves.

"Luc," she said with a smile and stood up to embrace him in a brief hug. "You look well."

He felt it too. "Thank you." He walked around his desk as she sat back down. "Is everything okay? You? The kids?"

"We're all fine. Well, as fine as we can be." She forced a smile, but sadness darkened her features. It had been three months since she lost Alan, and though Lucas had experienced the loss of his parents, he could hardly imagine how it must feel to lose the one person you truly loved—your soul mate. That was who Alan had been to Rosemary. They had been each other's everything.

Lucas instinctively slid his hand inside his jacket and gently brushed his fingers against the edge of the folded envelope. He had never really thought about it before. Someone to call a partner—a husband—was not something he had believed to be part of his future. He had Municipal and deals, money and investments. He had the house, the car, and the cell phone. Why wasn't that enough anymore?

"What brings you up here?" he asked, snatching back his hand as if the paper had burned him.

"My signature was needed to release his pension. I've

kind of put it off for long enough now." She tightened her hold around the coordinated red handbag she held in her lap and tried to distract herself by looking around the large office.

"Are you taking the lump sum?" It wouldn't be much, maybe forty thousand, but it would go a long way to help. There was still a mortgage on the house, kids to get through to the end of college, and bills to pay.

Rosemary nodded. "They wanted me to take a smaller sum and leave it in, but…" She looked sadly at him. "That was meant to be for our future. Me and Alan's." She smiled. "He used it as an excuse every time he was late for dinner or missed one of Patrick's games. They could keep it all if—"

"I know." There was nothing else to say.

Taking a calming breath, Rosemary stood up. "I should go." She made her way toward the door. Stopping, she turned around and looked at Lucas with the warm motherly fondness he had grown accustomed to. "In thirty years of working here, he never thought as much about anyone as he did you." Pulling open the door, she said, "Promise me something?" When Lucas didn't answer she continued. "Don't be like Alan."

A lump formed in Lucas's throat and he couldn't find the words. Instead, he simply nodded.

"Take care," she said, and with that, she made her way toward the elevators.

Lucas sat back in his chair and felt the burn of confusion and anxiety turn over in his stomach and surge upward, hitting the back of his tongue. He just needed to take a step back for a moment and look at this rationally.

No. He pulled his cell phone out and quickly navigated through his contacts. This required a sound head and voice of reason. Okay, more like someone that believed in fate and dreams and love.

"Luc." Tasha sounded surprised as she picked up the call. "Hi. You okay?"

"Help," he said seriously. "I'm screwed." He could imagine the raised eyebrow and the pouting full lips of his sister as she tried to figure out what the hell was up with her usually sensible-headed brother.

"Erm, okay. How are you screwed exactly?"

Lucas looked toward his open office door. Quickly, he got out of his seat and went to close it. "I was this close to doing it."

"Doing what?" She clearly didn't remember telling him to stay with Dylan.

"Resigning."

"You resigned!" Her voice rose to an incredulous point.

"No. No, I was there in Oscar's office and I was going to but then he offered me the West Coast." Tasha was silent. She obviously had no idea how amazing the offer had been. "It's like everything I ever wanted." He paused. "What I wanted," he said. He listened to the words he just repeated and came to a realization. It was what he *had* wanted, but not anymore.

"Luc?"

"I'm going to resign." There, he had said it and he meant it. A new sense of calm and relief washed through him and suddenly the uncertainty of his future made him smile.

There was a giddy scream down the phone and Lucas listened to Tasha's excited babble. "And, what next? What are you going to do?"

Lucas chewed thoughtfully at his lip. He knew what he hoped to do. But he had to be sure of one more thing. "You are happy, aren't you? You're okay—"

"Go to him." She already knew.

"But—"

"But nothing, Luc. You don't have to keep looking out for me. Not anymore. That's Liam's job now. It's time you did something for yourself." He had always been working to secure her future. There had never been anyone else. It had all been for her.

"You don't think it's insane?"

Tasha laughed. "It's completely insane, but that's what makes it so fantastic. He said it, right? He said he loved you?"

Had he? Lucas wasn't so sure. Making love and being in love were two different things, weren't they? "I don't know."

"Do you love him?"

He smiled into the phone. "Yes," he confessed. Holy hell, what had he just said?

"Then that's all that matters."

"But what if?"

"What? Things don't work out?" she said.

Lucas nodded to the empty office.

"Then I'll be waiting for you when you come home. Luc, I'm only going to say this once. I love you, but sometimes you can be the biggest idiot out there."

Gee, thanks.

"Stop worrying about me and do what makes you happy."

I'm scared. "I love him."

"Then go and be with him, because from what I saw, he loves you too."

It was like she had lit a fire in his heart. "Thank you."

"You do realize I expect free vacations for life if things work out, yeah?"

Lucas laughed. "Sure. Talk to you later."

"Bye."

He pocketed his cell and took the envelope from his jacket. This was maybe the first really sensible thing he had ever done.

WAITING FOR DYLAN TO ANSWER WAS ALMOST LIKE torture. He could imagine now, the old Nokia spinning on Dylan's bedside, alone and abandoned as it vibrated for no one but its own entertainment. His mind drifted from Dylan's cell phone to the man himself. Dressed in board shorts and an open shirt and walking along the beach, sea spraying up and around him as a breeze blew back his sun-bleached hair. Oh damn. Shifting in his seat, Lucas tried to stem the attraction that had shot straight to his groin. What just thinking about the man could do to him.

"Hello?" A gruff voice came over the phone and Lucas's chest ached, but in a good way.

"Hey," Lucas said. "Sorry, were you sleeping?" He looked at his watch. It was a little after ten in the morning, which made it one in the afternoon there.

Dylan mumbled something Lucas didn't make out, but

it was accompanied by one of the cutest sleepy sounds he thought he had ever heard. The sweet whimper eventually turned into a more coherent sentence. "Was up late celebrating," he uttered and Lucas listened to the crumpled sound of him turning over in bed.

Jealousy swept through Lucas. He wanted to be right there in bed with Dylan enjoying the lazy afternoon. "It's all signed and official then?"

"Yup... well, good as." He started to sound a little more awake. "I had an Apple Mojito for you," he said and chuckled. "Or maybe three."

Damn, even over the phone the man was hot. "Sounds fun."

"Yeah. They're good people." Dylan groaned sleepily and Lucas imagined him stretching his body out from beneath the bed sheets. "What can I do you for?" Dylan asked. "I assume you weren't just missing the sound of my voice."

"Well, now you mention it, I have missed it. It's very sexy." All silky-south and sun-drenched.

Dylan gave a throaty laugh and in a low voice said, "I miss you too."

Oh God. Leaning forward, Lucas scooted his chair further under his desk and ran a hand down to his crotch. He was so fucking hard, and his insanity must be heightening because for a split second, he actually contemplated knocking one out right here in his office. He so needed to call Dylan when he was home and in the privacy of his own bedroom.

Okay, focus. "Are you okay to talk?" He needed Dylan to be serious for a moment.

"Sure," Dylan said, the playfulness falling away from his voice. "Is everything okay? Are you okay?" He knew about the meds and the doctors and he was obviously concerned.

"I'm fine." Lucas paused. *Shit*. "I've done something stupid. Well, not stupid as such but…"

"Okaaay," Dylan said slowly.

"I don't want to sound like super crazy or anything. But I was hoping maybe… And you can say no if you want to, but I really hope you won't."

"Okay," Dylan said again.

He had Dylan's attention. Just like he'd had Oscar's attention only moments before. "So, I just resigned and I kind of want to run something by you."

There was a surprised sound on the other end of the phone and Lucas felt the confidence to continue with his proposition. Oh yes. He definitely had Dylan's attention now.

Epilogue

Four months later…

"Just put them over there," Dylan said and pointed to the far side of the dock. He eyed the box of ceramic pumpkin candle holders and suddenly felt like he was in some freaky twilight zone.

A Halloween-themed wedding on a tropical island—people were weird. Maybe if it had been his fifth or sixth or even second freaking wedding on the island, Dylan might not have minded. But the new season of visitors and vacationers started in less than a week, his first in charge of Sapphire Cay, and he already had feelings of doubt and had started getting stressy over things like napkins. Yes, fucking napkins. And heaven help anyone that brought up cutlery and the need to have more than one knife and one fork on a table or, even more so, the fact they needed to match.

"Has my witch made it ashore yet?"

Dylan looked over his shoulder and did his best not to glare at the wedding planner—*his* wedding planner. "You mean the six foot hag I sent to the dining room?" And then he smiled and the urge to maim and stab something or someone eased a little.

Edward rolled his eyes only the way Edward could. "That's the bint," he said in his cultured British tones and laughed. "Ugly thing if you ask me. But it's what the bride and groom wanted. You Americans and your crazy thing for Halloween." He shook his head as he picked up one of the boxes containing black soft furnishings and headed back along the dock. "Don't ever do this to me again."

Closing his eyes, Dylan enjoyed the cool spray swept up from the ocean by the gentle breeze. This was what it was all about—sharing this peace and beauty with others. He opened his eyes and smiled as he spotted Lucas heading down the beach. Something else he would never get tired of. In a loose-fitting white T-shirt and cutoff jeans, Lucas looked amazing.

"Hey," he called, waiting as Lucas made it to the dock and into his arms. He buried his face in Lucas's hair and breathed in the soap and sea smell of his lover.

"I missed you," Lucas said and squeezed his arms around Dylan's waist. "Don't you have staff that can do this stuff for you so we can stay in bed all day?" He teasingly pressed his thigh into the space between Dylan's legs.

Dylan laughed. Lucas looked exactly as he had left him that morning, blissed out from sex and well rested. "Later," he whispered and caught Lucas's mouth with his in a firm kiss. "Things to do."

"I know," Lucas said and looked up at the cloud-spattered sky. "Rain's coming."

Dylan looked up and smiled. "Maybe it'll blow right over." He met Lucas's eyes and his chest swelled. Lucas looked so good and happy, and he wanted nothing more than to spend every waking minute wrapped up in this man's arms. He was interrupted from his appreciation by Lucas's sharp intake of breath and he gasped too as warm rain switched from a light drizzle to pouring heavily on them. He held Lucas close, cupping his face as he kissed him in the rain. He didn't care about being wet, and he ignored the squeals and frantic movement of his staff as they ran for cover. Instead, he stood exactly where he was with everything he cared about in that one place—this island and this man.

Hugging Lucas close, Dylan rested his chin on Lucas's shoulder and thought about all the reasons he was happy he had finally settled down. As he lifted his arm, his tattoo caught Lucas's attention.

Lucas traced the tattoo and he repeated the words inscribed there, "Follow the sun." He looked up at Dylan with an easy smile and a spark in his eyes. Though their paths had been different, it was that small mantra that had brought them both to this point. Without it, Lucas might not have dared to take a chance on Dylan and life, and God knows where Dylan might have ended up. Certainly, not here in the arms of the man he couldn't imagine being without.

"I love you," he whispered against Lucas's mouth and ran his hands back through Lucas's hair, shaking away the water as the rain shower stopped just as quickly as it started.

Lucas looked up at him through his lashes, droplets of water catching the sunlight as he blinked and they fell to his cheeks. "I love you too."

READ THE NEXT BOOK IN SAPPHIRE CAY - UNDER THE SUN

Under The Sun (Sapphire Cay 2)

When hate turns to love, the Marine and the wedding planner will find their happy ending.

Edward McAllister, wedding planner extraordinaire, arrives at Sapphire Cay for a wedding. He has four days to go until the big day, but his careful plans are foiled when he spots someone destroying the stage he was setting. It doesn't matter that the guy pulling down the old pavilion and digging trenches is hot – he's messing with Edward's OCD, and Edward isn't afraid to let the sexy marine know precisely how he feels.

Forced out of the military after he was injured, Jamie Durand returns to the place he once called home to recuperate and rethink his life. With every one of his dreams shattered, he can't see a way out, but when the hotel's prissy wedding planner dislikes him at first sight, Jamie makes it his mission to get the man to like him. Only like turns to lust, and with that, love is never far away.

Boyfriends for Hire

Boyfriends For Hire

1. Darcy
2. Kaden
3. Gideon
4. Jared
5. Felix
6. Caleb

Standalone Christmas

- The Road to Frosty Hollow

Also from RJ & Meredith

Standalone Christmas

- <u>The Road to Frosty Hollow</u>

Free Reads

- Stronger Together

Meet RJ Scott

RJ discovered romance in books at a very young age and realized that if there wasn't romance on the page, she could create it in her head. With over one hundred and fifty books published, she is a full time author of gay romance.

She lives and works out of her home in the beautiful English countryside, spends her spare time reading, watching films, and enjoying time with her family.

The last time she had a week's break from writing she didn't like it one little bit and has yet to meet a box of chocolates she couldn't defeat.

www.rjscott.co.uk | rj@rjscott.co.uk

NEWSLETTER - rjscott.co.uk/rjnews

facebook.com/author.rjscott

instagram.com/rjscott_author

amazon.com/author/rj-scott

bookbub.com/authors/rj-scott

goodreads.com/rjscott

patreon.com/RJScott

Meet Meredith Russell

Meredith Russell lives in the heart of England. An avid fan of many story genres, she enjoys nothing less than a happy ending. She believes in heroes and romance and strives to reflect this in her writing. Sharing her imagination and passion for stories and characters is a dream Meredith is excited to turn into reality.

www.meredithrussell.co.uk
meredithrussell666@gmail.com

facebook.com/meredithrussellauthor
x.com/MeredithRAuthor
instagram.com/miss_meredith_r